INTERGIRL:
A Hard
Currency
Hooker

INTERGIRL: A Hard Currency Hooker

by Vladimir Kunin

Translated from the Russian by
Antonina W. Bouis

BERGH PUBLISHING, INC.
276 Fifth Avenue, New York, N.Y. 10001

© 1991 by BERGH PUBLISHING, Inc.
Paper ISBN 0-930-267-07-9
Case ISBN 0-930-267-06-0

Manufactured in the United States of America

Sales and distribution: The Talman Company, Inc.
150 Fifth Ave, NY, NY 10011 Tel (212)620-3182
Fax (212)627-4682

Introduction

Intergirl: A Hard-Currency Hooker, a novel by Vladimir Kunin, offers Western readers a glimpse of a little-known aspect of life in the Soviet Union—the special world of hard-currency prostitutes. "Intergirls" are a uniquely Soviet phenomenon: prostitutes who work only for hard currency, or *valuta,* which only foreigners are allowed to have. The ruble is not a freely convertible currency and possession of *valuta* is a criminal offense for Soviet citizens.

However, *valuta* buys things that rubles cannot—there are special hard-currency stores, called Beriozkas, that carry a wide range of goods, from groceries to fur coats and blenders and TVs for sale only for dollars, francs, marks, and schillings.

There are two official exchange rates for rubles inside the USSR. The first is for shopping at Beriozkas and hotels: $1.65 to the ruble. This is very far removed from the soaring black market rate, which had reached over 15 rubles to the dollar by the summer of 1990. In November 1989, the Soviet government introduced a special conversion rate for tourists of six rubles to the dollar, but only for buying with rubles. Wherever the currency is hard, the stiffer exchange rate prevails.

It is almost impossible to give dollar equivalents for ruble amounts, because so many things are subsidized by the state—rents are very low, about 15 rubles a month, bread and milk cost only a small fraction of a ruble, a school uniform about 20 rubles. So a salary of 150 rubles a month does not seem bad. Unless you want to purchase a pair of winter boots, which can cost 300 rubles, or any other luxury item.

The Intergirls, who work with Intourists, or foreign tourists, have a specialized profession. They speak several languages and keep up on international news—sort of free-lance geishas. Their activity is frowned upon by the police, of course, but since there is no law against prostitution in the USSR, they must be arrested and sentenced under other articles of the Criminal Code. There is no law against prostitution in the USSR because the Soviet state declared that prostitution did not exist, could not exist, in a perfect socialist society.

Article 88—currency violation (Possession of *valuta* and exchanging it for rubles on the black market)—is a favorite for punishing Intergirls. A division of the internal police, a vice squad for Intourists, deals with the girls and their clients. The whole system is corrupt, from top to bottom. The girls, in order to get near their customers, must first get into the hotels and restaurants which are off limits to Soviet citizens. That means bribing doormen, maitre d'hotels, waiters, and floor ladies. All these people are involved in a hypocritical system, but the book's point is that the prostitutes are the real victims of this system.

The novel was an enormous best-seller in the Soviet Union when it came out in 1987. It was an even greater hit as a film two years later. Its popularity inside the Soviet Union was due to several factors: it was the first to deal with such a sexy topic so matter-of-factly, showing the profession through the eyes of a practitioner.

Secondly, it was an expose of the whole hard-currency versus ruble inequity, raising an issue whose injustice has rankled for years.

Thirdly, it showed Soviet life in the West. Tanya, the heroine, became an Intergirl in order to catch a foreign husband and move away with him. Her life in Sweden sounds fascinating to Soviet readers who have never been abroad. Her life in Leningrad should be fascinating to American readers who have never been to the Soviet Union or whose trips have not revealed this side of Soviet reality to them.

AWB

PART

I

It was the middle of one of summer's white nights. I had to get dressed, fix myself up, slip out of the hotel, find a taxi, get home, sleep a few hours, and be at my hospital by eight.

I still had plenty of time. I was at the open window wearing shoes and panties, fastening my bra without hurrying. I knew that I looked terrific even without any clothes on and I was sure that he couldn't take his eyes off me now. But while I feel something for men in the evening, by morning I'm so sick of it I couldn't tell you. So my unhurried movements were merely habit.

From the height of the tenth-floor hotel room I saw a tug and a barge with yellow sand on the Neva River. When the puffing tug crawled under the halves of the Litenyi Bridge flung upward into the sky and the sound of its engine was almost inaudible, a song from an old movie came from the barge. Who the hell knew what movie . . .

"I love you, Tanya," he said behind me.

He spoke Russian pretty well. Even got a bonus from his company for knowing the language.

"Me too," I replied without turning. He was interfering with the song from the barge.

"I want to get married with you," he said solemnly.

Goddamn it! Was this it? Was this the end?

I wheeled around to him. He was still lying in the narrow hotel bed, his myopic eyes in a tense squint.

"Thank the Lord!" I even laughed. "You've cracked at last."

"What?"

I sat down on the bed and caressed his face. "Is it true that we will get married?"

I've noticed that I always use a simplified vocabulary with him and other foreigners who speak Russian. I do it unconsciously. Maybe my instinct is to make dealing with me easy.

"Do you really want to marry me?"

"Yes." He put his head on my lap. His hair was soft and thin with ash gray streaks. "I've already talked with my papa and mama."

This was getting serious.

"No, honest?"

"Yes, of course."

"And we'll go live in your country?"

"Yes. If you want."

He had to ask! Why else was I here? They don't understand us at all. Even the smartest ones.

I bent over and kissed his cheek. I smelled his stale breath, got up, and said carefully, "Everything will be the way you want it now." And I went into the bathroom.

I pulled on my Deutsche dress—had to give Kisulya five hundred for it—packed up all my make up and put on some lipstick. And I saw his unwashed shaving brush with dried soap suds in the bristles. I've been screwing him for a month and every time I saw that unwashed brush. But until now I had felt that it was his business. But today . . . I washed it out, dried it on the towel, and set it on the glass shelf in front of the mirror. Maybe my new life would begin with that brush.

I came out of the bathroom and looked at the Neva through the window. But the sand barge was gone —only its wake spreading out in weak waves in the water.

"Here's five hundred crowns." He looked at me over his glasses and handed me the money. "As usual. But if you want it in dollars it will be less. The exchange rate has dropped a bit on the dollar, and that might not be good for you."

Should I take it? Or not? . . . The hell with those five hundred crowns! I had something much more important. So I said, "Put it away. Forget it. Now you know what you'll be with me? A freebie."

I could see he didn't understand a thing.

"In our country wives don't take money from their husbands for . . . for that," I explained with unwitting pride in our national mores. "It's immoral."

"That is correct. Although a wife is always more expensive." He put the money back in his wallet.

They're such careful and calculating guys! Not like our men. Though I don't even know if I like that or not.

5

"Will you take presents?" He had bought me a few things at the hard currency Beriozka store.

I looked at my watch and decided not to risk it. What if I got grabbed by the special services boys, and they saw the stuff, it would take forever to explain that I hadn't stolen it . . . and I'd be late for work.

"No. Why don't you bring them to me yourself? All right?"

"All right," he agreed. "And your mother we have to tell about us, also."

His Russian made me laugh.

"Absolutely! Ciao." I kissed his nose and went to the door. "God speed!"

We no longer have *dezhurnyas,* or floor ladies, at Intourist hotels. They've made it like hotels "out there." But who can keep a senior maid from sitting by the elevator? No one.

And so our dear sweet Anna Matveyevna was sitting at the desk. She looked fine for half a century. All dressed in Lurex with a beehive hairdo.

"Good morning, Anna Matveyevna."

"Tanya!" You'd think she was my own mother.

I called the elevator, slipped her a ten, and added a French lipstick. Anna Matveyevna batted her eyelashes. "Oh, you're always too much, Tanya! Gosh, I just don't know . . ."

The elevator came. I waved to her and slipped into the cabin.

And while I looked at myself in the mirror and imagined myself "over there" as his wife, Anna Matveyevna (what a bitch!) picked up the telephone . . .

Of course, by the time I got to the lobby they were waiting for me. I was so upset I spat.

"Ptooey!" I said. "What is this crap, Zhenya?"

Zhenya was there in a sweater and leather jacket, yawning away. He was recently promoted to lieutenant. He was always the junior man.

"Why don't you let me go this time, huh, Zhenya?"

"Be serious, Zaitseva! Let's go, come on. We're so bored without you at the station . . ."

We went. What else could I do?

"Anna Matveyevna snitched?" I asked.

"This isn't like you, Tanya," Zhenya said sadly. "You're an experienced woman. A pro. What silly questions."

We went down the hotel corridors. Stuffed easy chairs, polished wood, ashtrays everywhere. Another world! It looked as if the hotel was sleeping its head off, when actually, you had to keep your wallet open: our "union" was working, and the special services were on alert, and all kinds of cheap traders were wandering about. . . .

"I'm getting married, Zhenya."

"Congratulations." Zhenya lets me go through the door. "Go on, Zaitseva."

Every time I walk into that crummy room, with horrible desks, the torn couch, the black chairs, and the ugly safe, I think that this room was taken out of some station house and plunked down in the middle of the luxurious Intourist Hotel, built to the latest technological specifications. Every time it's a change of worlds for me.

"Hi," I said to everyone present.

"The best people of our union," Tolya said with a smile. "Practically the whole team now. Sit down, Tatyana Nikolayevna."

Tolya is the senior squad commander for our hotel.

7

There's nothing of the police captain about him. In suit and tie he looks like a graduate student. But his glasses are more expensive than any student could buy. Real high-fashion glasses!

In the middle of the room is a barricade made up of two desks in a T. Along one wall were seven chairs for suspects.

On the first was Natasha the Schoolgirl. A mean chick, obnoxious. Just sixteen. She hit the streets in eighth grade. Now she's in tenth. Dumb face—what do men fall for? She'll lie down under any drunken Finn for a hundred fifty of his stinking marks.

But beyond her is a parade of the elite! The Soviet fashion house had no business here. Vogue, Burda Moda, Nickerman, Quille, Cardin, Nina Ricci. . . .

Every suit was a thousand or two. The boots cost six or seven hundred. The cosmetics—Max Factor, Chanel, Christian Dior. . . . Not your Natasha the Schoolgirl stuff. This was our trade union. Intergirls. Valuta prostitutes. Hard currency hookers.

There's Zina Meleiko. She gets the best clients. Speaks Italian and Finnish. She put together a Swedish-Russian conversation book. On our topic. Many beginners borrowed it to copy. For twenty-five rubles. Not expensive. Just can't let her drink—she gets mean. She was high now. . . .

My best friend—Sima Gulliver. She was a champion volleyball player. She's one tough cookie! Can make any client pay a full hundred dollars. Won't go for less. When she puts on her makeup, you can't take your eyes off her. Got a brain like the whole Supreme Soviet. Can make money off anything.

Nina Kisulya. One businessman after the other, and

she's always in good shape. Swims in the morning, then the tennis courts, lunch only with business partners. Work in the evening. English, German, Finnish, of course . . . the Leningrad specialties. I respect Kisulya a lot. She and Gulliver brought me out into the world the first time.

And behind the desk—on the other side of the barricades—are the "specials." Three of them today. All in civies, of course, looking quite decent. The only place they're in their cop uniforms is their ID photographs. They're about our age, from twenty-four to thirty. All educated. Some graduated from universities, others from polytechs, others from phys. ed. institutes. And a few police courses. And they did the right thing! You get two twenty a month right off with your epaulets. That's not your crummy one forty as an engineer or teacher. Tolya gets two ninety as a captain. Not a gold mine, of course, but it's something. They all have children. Some have two.

"Sit down, sit down, Tatyana Nikolayevna. I'll continue with our game here." Tolya brought the paper right up to his eyeglasses. "Where did we stop? Oh, yes . . . 'I promise to go to school, to finish tenth grade, and get my certificate. . . .' "

"In sexual maturity," Zina Meleiko interrupted. She was way over the limit.

"Zina Vasilyevna, you're interrupting," Tolya said reproachfully and stuck his nose back in the paper. " 'Besides which, I give my word of honor as a Komsomol member not to visit the Intourist Hotel and never be a prostitute again.' Natasha, who wrote this a week ago?"

"All right, I did." The Schoolgirl stared at the ceiling brazenly.

9

"How many times now? I have a collection of these promises."

Natasha said nothing. She popped some gum in her mouth and started chewing, the cow. She's as pushy as a tank! Just then two uniformed cops peeked into the room. From the Territorial Division.

"Good day, comrade captain. We're here."

"Hi," Tolya said. "Have a seat in the hall. Yevgeny Alexeyevich, write up the charges on this overdeveloped child of the century. And we'll take a look to see how she manages. . . ."

He opened Natasha's passport and a photo of some darkie slipped out.

"Who's this?"

"My friend from Cambodia," the Schoolgirl replied with more animation. "He fights for peace. There's even an inscription on the back."

"Were you fighting for peace in his hotel room?"

"Yes."

Usually when the "specials" are hassling one of us, the rest keep quiet—we're on opposite sides of the desk. But this time even we laughed. What a bint!

Tolya rummaged in Natasha's stuff and began taking a pack of Rothman's apart. He spilled out the cigarettes and found a Finnish hundred mark bill between the cardboard and the foil. What a cretin! Who hides things that way! Amateur!

"We've never found more than fifty marks on you before, and this is a hundred," Tolya said in surprise.

"Everything is getting more expensive." Natasha blew a bubble.

"Cheap shit," Zina said angrily.

"Zina Vasilyevna!" Tolya looked at Zina over his glasses

and then turned to the Schoolgirl. "Since when did Cambodians pay in Finnish marks?"

"I found the marks."

"Lucky, aren't you? Where?"

"In the elevator."

"And naturally, you were on your way to us to turn the find in to the state budget, weren't you?"

"Naturally."

Now we all laughed out loud again.

Zhenya said, "I can see the headline in *Pioneer Pravda*. 'Honest Girls Act Like This.' The text: 'A girl from class 10B . . .'"

"Right," Zina said.

". . . turned in one hundred Finnish marks to the state, which she found . . ."

"In the pants of a famous Cambodian peace fighter," Zina said.

"Cut out the fun," Tolya said softly, and that was dangerous. We knew that very well. But Zina didn't catch on because she was drunk.

"Why not? We just started!"

"And we just finished," Tolya said even more quickly. "Let's start customs inspection. Everything out of your pockets and purses onto the table."

The usual thing. No one ever makes a fuss. You put out the whole thing—makeup, money, brand name cigarettes, lighters, notebooks, condoms, birth control pills, scented wipes. . . . All kinds of things in a woman's purse! Well, then they frisk you. That's why they're criminal investigators. You're not risking a thing. Even if they find valuta on you. "A gift." Or as that underage idiot said, "Found it in the elevator." They'll confiscate it, and that's it.

But Zina Meleiko (she was way over her limit) suddenly decided to demand her rights. She's as careful as a fox when she's sober, and here she said, "Where's your search warrant?"

Tolya looked at her and then said, "Mikhail Mikhailovich, please finish frisking Zina Vasilyevna and then arrest her for being at the Intourist Hotel after 11:00 P.M. in a drunken state."

Misha began filling out yet another form on Zina.

"Where do you work?"

"Same as last time. Leningrad Bridge Construction."

"Position?"

"Handywoman."

Her clothes were worth about two thousand, not counting the diamonds in her ears, which were worth a lot more. Zina doesn't wear cheap stuff.

"What is your salary?"

"Ninety rubles."

"Look how the standard of living for the working woman has grown!" Zhenya exclaimed. "It's enough to take one look at Zina Vasilyevna Meleiko to show up all the hostile propaganda for just that, to shut up all the lying voices and make them weep with frustration."

A policeman looked in.

"We're holding the car, Anatoly Andreyevich."

"All right, I'm done. Take these two."

"And the chain of illegalities begins," Zina snorted drunkenly.

"If I had a law against prostitution, Zina Vasilyevna, I'd have put you away years ago," Tolya said softly.

Zina laughed. "If you needed to, you'd have gotten rid of all of us in two weeks without any law. Across the country. But we're still running around free. That means you need us!"

"We need you?" Misha was outraged. "We're the Special Service of the Criminal Investigation Department, our duty is to protect the property, life, and health of foreign citizens, guests of our country, and we're forced to spend half our working hours on your protected activity! And you say we need you?"

"Well, not you," Zina said. "Maybe your bosses. . . . Or someone else."

"Come along, come along," the uniformed cop said in fright.

"Right. Ciao, kids. See you tomorrow." Zina gave the chewing Natasha the Schoolgirl a shove. "Go, babe. And don't chomp near my ear, you filthy minor."

"The difference is only in the age and the price," the Schoolgirl said with a smile and blew a bubble gum bubble in farewell. The bubble burst and the door closed behind it.

Tolya sat down at the desk and looked through Kisulya's stuff.

Zhenya started on my purse, Misha on Gulliver's makeup kit.

"How much money?" Tolya asked Kisulya.

"I don't remember. Around twelve hundred."

Gulliver and I looked at each other. That meant that Kisulya had handled three guys at a hundred greens each and had time to do the "one to four." That Kisulya sure works fast. High class stuff!

Tolya read our minds. "High class! You've had three clients at a hundred dollars each and you've managed to exchange the valuta for rubles at four to one! Well, Nina Petrovna?"

13

"Anatoly Andreyevich, what valuta are you talking about! This is my own personal Soviet money. Ever since apartment burglaries have gone up, I've been carrying my valuables with me."

"Haven't you heard that street robberies have gone up?" Misha asked.

"Be serious, Misha! You know that I don't use public transportation and I frequent only the finest places. It's my life savings."

"What about a savings account?" Zhenya asked.

Sima Gulliver and I knew for a fact that Kisulya had at least a hundred thou somewhere. But you couldn't catch Kisulya salting her tail.

"Zhenya! What savings account? Where would I get money? Everyone knows what a spendthrift I am. I like to dress well, I support several pimps. . . . How could I have an account?"

"And why do you have so many condoms, Serafima Arkadyevna?"

"Why not?" Sima Gulliver had been quiet a long time and now she wanted to gab. "Haven't you heard about the AIDS epidemic beyond the borders? You can only get it by . . . You know . . . sexual means, excuse the expression. So we're working hand-in-hand with our Soviet health services. And in the future, Anatoly Andreyevich, I would ask you to keep that in mind most seriously."

"Serafima Arkadyevna, don't you remember that we warned you most seriously last time to at least keep away from government delegations?" Tolya asked.

And I realized that we would get out of this okay.

"I never see them! Anatoly Andreyevich! I don't deal with the government level at all now, and I don't give a good goddamn about those government delegations! Even though they're people too and need to relax . . ."

"And who serviced the Argentines today?"

"Slander. Anatoly Andreyevich, I swear to you, it's slander. I didn't even think about the Argentines! Not a single Argentine! I didn't even come close to them." She sighed and asked in this innocent little girl way, "But tell me, dear Anatoly Andreyevich, how do I keep them from coming close to me?"

"Take your things. What does Zaitseva have, Yevgeny Alexeyevich?"

"Zaitseva's getting married, and so everything's fine with her."

"Yes," I said. "Today's the last time I'm partying with you, my friends . . ."

"Who's the lucky man?" Misha asked.

I laughed.

"You should know your job, Mikhail Mikhailovich," Tolya said. "Edward Larsson, representative of Belitronics, manufacturers of robotics. In Leningrad as part of the Swedish delegation to the international trade show. Tatyana Nikolayevna was handed over to him by Gunwald Rein, also of the same company, her client last year, who couldn't marry our Tanya because he turned out to be a faithful husband to his Swedish wife and a loving father of three children. And what's even better, Tatyana Nikolayevna. Mr. Rein is a potential wino, while Edward Larsson is quiet, dependable, and a bachelor, obviously going to move up in his firm."

Everyone, the cops and my girlfriends, laughed it up.

Even I giggled for a bit but then it hit me. (That happens sometimes. I suddenly stop thinking and calculating, and everything becomes hateful, and I don't give a shit.) It's gotten me into trouble lots of times.

"Good Lord!" I said. "I'm so sick of you. All of you!"

Not a single laugh. Dead silence.

Kudryavtsev took off his glasses, wiped them, and put them back on. And he said in a soft voice, not hiding his anger, "And we're sick of you. I've had it up to here with you!" He grabbed his throat. "You give off filth like rings on water. If I had my way. . . ."

He pulled himself together and said in a calm voice, "Yevgeny Alexeyevich, please show Tatyana Nikolayevna out. Since you're handling her today."

We went through the dark hallways. I pulled out a cigarette but couldn't find my lighter. I was shaking. Zhenya struck a match and lit my smoke. Brought me to the door.

The doorman Petr Nikanorovich—a retired shit—saw Zhenya and jumped up all sleepy from his couch and hurried to open the door, the bastard. The former lieutenant colonel bowed to the present lieutenant, rushing to show how hard he worked. Even though he takes three or five rubles from each prostitute to get into the hotel. And a ten from guests who want to get into the restaurant.

He saw me and acted surprised—how did she get in?—even though he'd gotten a fiver from me that evening, the scum.

"Goodbye, Tanya." Zhenya seemed to be apologizing.

I didn't reply. I couldn't speak. I nodded and left.

○

It was so wonderful outside! The air was clean and cool. . . . The city . . . What a knockout! The sun wasn't

16

up yet but the windows in the high floors were burning gold. Like a fairy tale! I couldn't describe how beautiful it was. I felt that I was about to sit down on the stone steps and start bawling.

"Where to?"

This old driver in a wheezing cab pulled up. I looked at his plates—from garage number 4.

"Twenty-eight, Science Prospect," I said.

"Apartment?"

"None of your business."

"A tenner."

"No problem."

"Get in."

I got in and we took off.

We were on the road. I pulled out a mirror, cotton, and cream to wipe my face. I always take my makeup off before I get home. Like morning exercises. Like moving from one state to another. And also not to upset my mother. She wouldn't say anything, of course, but . . . you have to protect your loved ones.

"Listen," the driver suddenly said, "I drove an American around for four hours on my last shift. To Pavlovsk and Pushkin, and all over the place. He didn't have enough of our wooden ones, and he paid the fare in greenbacks. You need some? I'll give you three to one."

You viper, I thought to myself! Is it written all over me? That he can offer me dollars without being afraid?

But I didn't bat an eyelash.

"Excuse me, please, but I don't understand what you're talking about."

"Wow!" he laughed. "You ought to be on stage!"

"You must be confusing me with someone else, comrade," I said.

17

He laughed even harder.

"No way!" he said. "Can't confuse you gals with any-one . . ."

We were pulling up to my building. Actually to the one next door, number thirty two.

Our block, like all new housing projects, had narrow little roads and we couldn't get around the huge Volvo refrigerator truck parked in front of us. It was from Sovtransauto, and made deliveries abroad. They know how to pull tricks, too. That truck was often here. One of their drivers must live in the neighborhood.

"All right, I'll get out here," I told the driver. "Stop."

I got out, put a tenner on his seat (the meter hadn't even reached three), took out a Marlboro, lit up, and said to the creep, "By the way. About the greenbacks. Article eighty-eight, paragraph one. Three to eight with confiscation."

"Give me a break!"

"You'll be begging the prosecutor for a break."

"And what article will they get you on?"

"There isn't one for me. This "social phenomenon" does not exist in our country. Get it, pops?"

The son of a bitch laughed. "Then, maybe you'll give me your phone number?"

"Out of your league," I said. "You wouldn't have enough wooden rubles or greenbacks. You'd lose your shirt. Ciao, bambino. Sorry."

And I went home.

The apartment was as black as a black man's belly. We always draw the curtains tight during the white nights. Otherwise you can't get any sleep.

I sat down on my mother's bed and couldn't see her.

"I'm getting married, Ma," I whispered.

"Thank God. Who is it?" Mama asked in a whisper, too, for some reason. She was still half asleep. I could tell from her voice.

"Edik. Edward Larsson."

"The tall one?"

"No. The tall one is Gunt. This is Edik. He picked me up here once, remember?"

"How will we all fit in here?"

"I'll live with him."

"Where?"

"In Sweden."

"Oh my God!" she whimpered. "What about me?"

She turned on the bed lamp. She was sitting there in her old pajamas, hair messed up, skinny. She clasped her hands near her chin and there was so much sadness and horror in her eyes.

○

I didn't get a minute's sleep. Mama got crazy and made me crazy, too, and then she tried to make me breakfast. I threw on a house dress and started making breakfast for her, pulling the tea pot and the matches out of her hands.

We knocked around the kitchen, bumping into each other at the stove, the refrigerator, the sink.

"What has your life been like?" I shouted at her. "A lousy husband and a salary of one forty? A one-room co-op? You call that life?"

"Why did you ever drop out of college?" Mama shouted and burned her hand on the frying pan.

I grabbed her hand, stuck it under cold water, and said, "Because I took the trolley to college and every morning I read the sign: 'Learn to be a trolley driver . . . Four months. Starting salary three hundred.' And I was supposed to study for five years in order to earn one ten. You know what you can do with college. You didn't get much out of yours!' "

"Yes I did!" Mama pulled away from me. "I bring up children, I'm a teacher!"

"They're the ones who educate you! Put down that plate, I'll do it myself!"

○

Later (I was dressed in jeans and a T-shirt and Mama had a bandage on her hand and had combed her hair

20

and calmed down a bit), we sat at our tiny table and ate breakfast.

"I want my own house, my own car! I want to go to the store and buy what I need instead of paying black marketeers triple price! I want to see the world. Different countries . . . Not on TV. With my own eyes. I want to touch things with my own hands instead of listening to TV personalities. They spend five years abroad, you practically have to dynamite them out, and then they come back and say nasty things. But if I sit here in this kitchen, I'll never see anything! All right, I'm no politician like Margaret Thatcher, or a mathematician like Sofia Kovalevskaya, or a cosmonaut like Valentina Tereshkov. . . . But I have something else, Mama! Believe me. I'm a woman. So why shouldn't I . . ."

"But Tanya! Dearest! That's selling yourself . . ."

"Right," I said calmly now. "Right, Mama. And who doesn't sell himself today? Who doesn't try to sell his profession and his talent for the highest price? Who doesn't want to be rewarded for his work? A writer haggles with the publishers, an artist sells his paintings, an engineer gets a fee for his invention."

"But books, inventions, and paintings bring people happiness! Physical and spiritual . . ."

"There you go!" I got angry again. "We're used to thinking globally—on the scale of the people, the continent, the cosmos! Nothing smaller. But what about the single individual!"

"Which individual?"

"Why, take Edward Larsson—a lonely Swedish engineer. If marrying me makes him spiritually happy (I can guarantee the physical part), isn't that something?"

"But why do you have to go so far away? Why doesn't

he move in with us? It'll be crowded at first, but then we'll trade for a bigger place."

"Mama! Just imagine this—an artist works many years on a painting and dreams that some day it will be noticed and appreciated. And when the painting is finished and he is offered a personal international exhibit, his mother says, 'No! No exhibits! It can hang right here in my kitchen!'"

"What are you talking about?"

"What's the difference? Damn it, why am I any worse than that?"

And Mama began to cry. I looked at the clock. I was late for work. But I couldn't leave her in this state.

"Calm down, Mama." I kissed her hand and she patted me automatically. "Calm down. I'll visit you several times a year. All our girls who marry aboard do that. That's the first thing. And the second, it's not going to happen for a while."

I looked at my watch, got up, put on an old jacket and began stuffing a few items of clothing into my big black bag. First of all, I had to take something for work—after all, I'd be away for twenty-four hours, and secondly, I had to stop by a marvelous place before work.

"But do you love him?" Mama asked hopefully.

I was so tired that I didn't have the energy to make anything up.

"Don't make me laugh, Ma. If I have to, I'll fall in love."

Fortunately, the bell rang just then. Mama jumped up from the table and hurried to the door.

"Sit," I said. "I'll get it. It's Lyalya, I'll bet."

Of course it was Lyalya, a former student of Mama's and our neighbor across the hall. She was eighteen.

Incredibly pretty! Last year she didn't pass the entrance exams into medical school and I got her a job as a nurse's aide at the hospital so that she could have a good work record.

"Hi," Lyalya said, imitating my voice. "Give me a break! I've been waiting and waiting . . ."

"Lyalya!" Mama was pleased to see her. "Hello, child!"

"Oh, I'm sorry, Alla Sergeyevna. Good morning."

"Mama, we're off."

"Wait!" Mama rushed into the room and came back, shoving two rubles at me. "Take it."

"I have money."

"You'll be gone overnight. You have to have a good meal."

"Mama, please . . ."

"Don't argue. And feed Lyalya too."

"Goodbye, Alla Sergeyevna."

"So long, Ma . . ."

Lyalya and I pulled up at the precinct house in a black Volga with antennas and a car telephone.

I could see the "perfect picture" from the car: Zina Meleiko in her evening war paint and extremely high heels was sweeping the courtyard with several old female winos, while the Schoolgirl on a rickety stepladder was washing the high first-floor windows. Two horrible-looking hags were helping her. Their faces were puffy and bruised. If you were to poke them, cheap rotgut would pour out of their ears!

"Hold it here, James," I said. "Lyalya, stay out of sight. I'll be right back!"

I took my bag and ran from the car. I pulled out jeans, a sweater, and a jacket from the bag and handed them to Zina.

"Turn your back!" Zina shouted at the elderly cop who was in charge of the whole crew.

The screw spat and turned around. Zina pulled on the jeans, took off the blouse, showing that she wasn't wearing a bra, and put on the sweater. Only then did she take off her skirt.

The winos laughed. Zina didn't even look in their direction. She lit up.

The Schoolgirl ran over and asked me for a cigarette. I gave her the finger and went back to the car.

O

When we reached the hospital I rummaged in my wallet among the big bills, took out a five, and paid the driver.

Lyalya said nothing in a huff until the staircase and then asked, "Why did you take two rubles from your mother? You have so much."

I love that Lyalya! What a fine girl! A real human being . . .

I hugged her as we walked. She tried to pull away, so I held her closer.

"Lyalya . . . Would it be better if she knew that I had money, and how much, and how I got it? Would it?"

"No."

"That's the point. You have to protect people."

Lyalya thawed and picked up the conversation we had begun in the car.

"Tanya! Why won't you take me with you sometime? How often do I have to ask?"

While Lyalya and I were driving to our hospital, six representatives of Belitronics in front of the hotel on the Neva were getting into a small orange company van that they had driven from Stockholm. The company name, address and telex number were on the sides.

"Who's driving today?" Benny asked.

Tall, red-faced Gunwald, with whom I hung around last year, shouted, "With whom can we entrust our precious lives in the foreign and hostile socialist environment? Who is the most decisive, the bravest, the best of us all?"

"Edward drives!" they shouted.

"Right!" yelled Gunwald. "A man who is marrying a Russian . . ."

He didn't get a chance to say "prostitute." Someone gave his jacket a tug from behind and he quickly changed to: ". . . Russian girl who deserves great respect! Even if she turns out to be a KGB agent!"

Everyone laughed. Edward smiled, got behind the wheel, and they headed for Vasilyevksy Island, to their exhibit.

O

My workday had started. My third world.

There was an electric clock on the wall over the TV in the department. Sometimes it seemed to me that I can see even the hour hand move. The minute hand spun like crazy for me.

Rear end, shot . . . Rear end, shot . . . Rear end . . .

"Hey, wait up . . . You've already got a huge hematoma here! Why don't I give you an injection in the hip this time? And we'll put a heater on your bum. . . ."

"Tanya! They're asking for you in Ward 3 . . . The little old lady by the window."

"On the way . . ."

"Tanya . . . My bandage is soaked through again."

"That's good. It means it's easing up. I'll change it."

"I've got such heartburn, Tanya. From everything, I mean it. And baking soda just makes it worse."

"Take this. Bourget powder."

"Tatyana Nikolayevna! Take Velikhova from Ward 7 up to X-ray."

"Here's a jar. Urinate in the morning before breakfast. And here's a box. For your stool. And write your surname here. So it doesn't get mixed up . . ."

"How can I do it into that little box?"

"Try using your head."

"Tanya, the stroke guy has to have his linens and robe changed. He's incontinent and. . . ."

"No problem! Lyalya! Get a clean change and come with me to Ward One. You'll help."

"What about lunch?"

"You'll have time. Hurry up."

"Tanya! Telephone! A very nice foreign accent."

And the clock seemed to stop. The hands just froze. "Hello? Edik?"

I had been at their expo so many times, at their Swedish section, that I could visualize him on the phone at his desk.

Cans of Tuborg on the desk, notes, catalogues. His co-workers, Gunwald Rein, Kenneth, and Benny, are also there. I heard their Swedish chatter, saw through the wide window part of the exhibit, and a huge crowd of our Leningraders wandering among the stands. Almost everyone of them had brochures and prospectuses in his hands . . .

"Tanya? It is I, Edward. Have you told your mama about us?"

"Of course! She's very, very happy!"

"I must pay her a visit."

"Of course!"

"I love you very much, Tanya. Today I will call the consulate and find out about your formalities and ours."

"All right. I kiss you."

"Thank you." He was silent and then hung up the phone carefully.

○

The minute hand went off on its run again. The hour hand moved more unhurriedly. My twenty-four shift was on its way.

"Patients, turn in your thermometers! What's the story with your temperatures?"

"Here's our bum. . . . Marvelous! Hold the cotton, you hold it . . ."

"Tanya, hey, Tanya! While you were away, Ivan Afanasyevich moaned for three days, he wouldn't let anyone sleep in the ward. And today he's terrific. He's in love with you, hee-hee!"

"He's stupid. Don't listen to him, Tanya."

"I love you too, Ivan Afanasyevich. Take this pill . . . Drink some warm water. If you want anything, just ring. All right?"

"Lyalya! You call this cleaning up? Do it over! All the corners, not a bit of dust! Why are the bed pans still full? Take them out and then scrub them! Do it right."

"God, I hope they don't bring anyone in for emergency today!"

"My dear patients! I'm turning the TV off in five minutes—and it's lights out!"

"Tanya, will you have tea with us?"

"Definitely, Vladimir Alexandrovich! Just let me put the light out in the wards."

"Tanya, here . . ."

"Goodness, where did those marvelous flowers come from?"

"They're for you. My mother brought them."

"Well thank you, my handsome little gentleman! Let me give you a kiss."

"Tanya, tea's ready!"

"Coming."

○

When I went into the orderlies' room, our traditional tea party was in full swing. Vysotsky was singing quietly (Lyalya always brings a tape with her), and our young doctor Vladimir Alexandrovich, Nina, the nurse from the next department, and old Sergeyevna, the other orderly, were there.

The electric teakettle was on the table, along with cabbage pies, cookies, the two-forty-a-kilo sausage, and tomatoes and cucumbers . . . Everyone who's on the twenty-four hour shift brings something from home.

I came into the room and felt my strength ebbing away. I pulled off my starched cap, tossed off my shoes, and padded around barefoot.

"Who's minding the store?" Vladimir Alexandrovich asked.

"No one," Nina replied. "Everyone's asleep. No one's very sick."

I took out my old black bag and got a bottle of Advocat, an egg cream liqueur, several packs of Dunhill, Rothmans, and Pall Mall, and two bars of Swiss chocolate.

"Let's live it up!" I said and collapsed on the couch.

Sergeyevna picked up the bottle and asked, "What's this?"

"It's sweet? Don't you remember, Tanya brought it once before? It's made with eggs," Nina told her.

"Oh, it's tasty!" Sergeyevna remembered.

"Where did you get all this, Tanya?" the doctor asked.

"From work." I didn't have the strength to make anything up.

"Moonlighting, are you?" Nina was jealous.

"Yep."

"Where?"

"At the Intourist." My bottle was already making the rounds.

"Also as a nurse?"

"A sister of mercy," I chuckled. "Lyalya, light me a cigarette and pour me a cup of tea. Let it cool off. I'll have a little nap. Haven't slept in two days."

"Well, let's drink," said Sergeyevna lifting her glass. "Tanya, will you have a drop?"

"Tanya doesn't drink, Sergeyevna! How many times do I have to tell you?" Lyalya said nervously.

"Here's to all the best." Sergeyevna gulped down half a tumbler.

"Look how some people live," Nina said. "And I was always wondering why Tanya insisted on working every third day."

Sergeyevna finished her glass.

"Have something to eat," the doctor ordered. "Or you won't last 'til morning."

He noticed that my cigarette had gone out and lit it with my own lighter.

"Do you like it?" I had seen him admiring it.

"Very much."

"Take it."

"I couldn't!"

"Take it, come on. A good-looking man should have good-looking things. Let's share one chocolate bar and the other . . . Sergeyevna! Take the second one for your granddaughter. The one with the puppies on the label."

"That's a good idea. All right." Sergeyevna put the chocolate in the pocket of her scruffy coat. "You're like an angel to us, Tanya."

I liked that so much, it woke me up.

"Who's left out?" I said. "Nina, take all the smokes. Just leave the open pack on the table. That should last 'til morning."

"Tanya! I can't tell you . . ."

"And you, Lyalya, take the package out of my bag. And try them on. I think they're your size."

Lyalya rummaged in my bag and came out with a package holding a pair of real Japanese running shoes. Everyone practically fainted! Except Sergeyevna, who said, "Nice slippers. Do your feet sweat in them?"

" 'Slippers?' " Nina couldn't believe it. "Are you kidding? . . . They're . . . they're . . ."

"A royal present," Vladimir Alexandrovich said with a smile.

Lyalya was dumbstruck. She just stood there, hugging the shoes to her chest.

"Happy birthday, Lyalya," I said wearily. "I wish you all the best. And that you get into college this year."

"Oh, that's right! Tomorrow's my birthday."

"Today," I corrected. "It's today already."

"Then we must have another drink." Sergeyevna reached for the bottle again.

But a patient wearing undershorts and a well-washed flannel bathrobe with a shawl collar appeared in the doorway.

"I'm sorry," he said, blinking in the bright light. "I think Ivan Afanasyevich is dead."

We jumped up, as if an explosion had shaken us.

That Ivan Afanasyevich sure gave us a run for the money!

We all tried to pull him through. But as soon as there was even a sign of hope, the old man would slip away from us again. Ivan Afanasyevich floated away to the other side, where no one needed a damn thing.

Then Volodya opened up his chest, picked up Ivan Afanasyevich's heart and . . . started massaging it. It kicked in, thank God.

Nina and I assisted, getting in the way like blind kittens. Lyalya was there, too. Sergeyevna bustled about. . . .

. . . We went from the operating room back to the ward. I was still barefoot, running alongside the trolley rolling the IV stand. Nina was fixing the oxygen mask. Vladimir Alexandrovich was watching the old man's pulse. We were all smeared with blood, our masks dangling from our necks. The patients were all out of bed. They were excited, poor things, and scared. And the runner in underwear was there, too.

" 'He's dead, he's dead!' You panicked, man," I said to him. "Everybody, back to bed!"

"Tanya, how about a date this evening?" Vladimir Alexandrovich asked me softly as we wheeled the patient. "We can go to my friend's house, watch a video . . ."

What a sturdy lad! He had just been bathing in live human blood, and now he wants to get under my skirt!

"Where were you before, Vladimir?" I said with a laugh, keeping my eye on the IV in Ivan Afanasyevich's arm. "Too late now. I'm getting married."

At five in the morning I was getting the medications ready for the morning shift. Lyalya ran in. Her eyes were popping, and she was looking all around, as if she had been sent on a mission by partisans. She ran over to me and started whispering.

"Hold on," I said. "They'll wait."

I got up, went to check on Ivan Afanasyevich, fixed the oxygen mask taped to his unshaven upper lip, reduced the drip rate on the IV, listened to his breathing, and went out. I stopped by Nina's post.

"Could you keep an eye on my guys? I'll be back in about ten minutes."

Lyalya was waiting on the stairs. She's got the curiosity of a cat.

"Can I come with you?"

"Fix your scarf. You look like a mess."

We went outside. Our hospital is very old. There's this gray courtyard, very St. Petersburg in style. And in the middle of the courtyard was a big blue car with its doors open. Kisulya at the wheel, all dolled up and fiddling with the radio knobs. Sima Gulliver was sitting next to her. She had stuck her long legs out the door and was smoking.

"Hi," I said. "What's up?"

"Hop in. Join the party." Kisulya pointed to the back seat.

Lyalya and I got in and lit up. Lyalya couldn't take her eyes off Kisulya and Gulliver. Of course, they were in the full regalia—real knockouts. Lyalya didn't even dream you could look like that.

Kisulya squinted carefully at Lyalya. I reassured her. "The child is theoretically prepared."

"Time to bring her out into the world, then," Gulliver said with a laugh.

"You'll manage without her," I said. "Any work?"

"Nah . . . a waste." Kisulya was annoyed. "I picked up a John in the hard currency bar, but he was so drunk he was useless. Waste of time."

"And lost the money?"

"She didn't," Gulliver said, laughing. "She got her hundred bucks. I'm the one who lost out. And how! You could die! . . . I gave Genka fifteen. He put me at the next table with a huge Frenchman. His ass came up over my head. Huge shoulders. Gorgeous face! . . . At three in the morning I've got him in a taxi, going to my place, and on the way he announces that women don't interest him and he likes only men. And if I could get him a man right away, he'd give me three hundred francs. Can you imagine! I said, 'You pathetic queer. I killed half the night on you . . . Pay me a no-show fee!' Alexei Petrovich, the driver from garage 2, was laughing so hard I thought he would hit something. Anyway, we turn around and I go back. So figure it out: five to get in, a ruble at the coat check, fifteen to Genka, four to Alexei Petrovich. All a loss."

Lyalya was holding her breath, listening to all this stuff. Time to wrap this up, I figured.

"What did you come to see me for?"

"We wanted to see our trade union's unique phenomenon. An Intergirl slaving away for the state."

"In her free time from work," Gulliver said, laughing.

"Every third day, and it's not dusty work. And it keeps things quiet."

"Who for?"

"Me. My mother. The 'specials.' Everybody."

"To each his own. We brought you a wedding present, Tanya."

"A special aid for export brides," Gulliver said and handed me a piece of paper folded in two.

I opened it and saw a list.

"What is it?"

"A list of the certifications and documents you need to leave the USSR. The order that they must be handed in and the official deadlines for making the decisions. For each piece of paper, can you imagine?"

"The slightest mistake, and you have to start from scratch. They kick you around from office to office. The way they did with Little Sveta and Manya the Button, remember?"

"They'll hold up your paperwork for three years . . . and you can forget Sweden! Do you know why the cops keep all this information hidden away?"

"Why?"

"To keep people inside."

"Okay. Where'd you get it?"

"Lettuce works wonders," Gulliver joked.

"What do I owe you?"

"Don't even think about it. We'll settle up. By the way, need a polar fox coat?"

"Size?"

"Yours."

"How much?"

"For you, a thousand bucks. Or, as our Moscow colleagues put it, a thousand grunigs."

"I don't have any valuta, thank God. What about in wooden rubles?"

"Four thou—and it's yours."

"Should I buy it for my mother? She doesn't have anything for the winter. Let's see it."

"It's in the back."

I turned around, picked up the bag, and pulled out a gorgeous Norwegian polar fox coat. Lyalya gasped.

"Out of the car," I said to her. "Try it on."

Lyalya got out. I handed her the coat. She put it on over her lab coat, pulled off her kerchief, and loosened her hair over her shoulders.

The coat was excellent. But Lyalya in the coat made the three of us fall down. And this despite the fact that she was wearing hospital slippers and was surrounded by the peeling plaster walls of the courtyard, littered with all kinds of crap.

"Wow, what a girl!" Kisulya said.

"Major competition growing up!" Gulliver said, shaking her head.

"Just try it," I told them and shouted at Lyalya, "Come on, come on, take it off. You're too young to get a taste for that kind of stuff."

Lyalya reluctantly took off the coat and handed it to me. I put it back in the bag and said to Kisulya, "I'll take it. I don't know when I'll have money again. And I have to take care of my mother for the winter."

"Okay," Kisulya said with a casual nod. "When you bring the lettuce, you can have the coat. Agreed?"

"Fine. Thanks, girls." I got out of the car too.

"Enjoy it."

"Tanya! Don't lose the list," Gulliver called after me. "Pay particular attention to the first point. Without it you can't even apply to the Wedding Palace. You have to start at the Swedish consulate."

My God! If I only had understood Swedish then the way I do now.

Edik and I were in the General Consul's office, a middle-aged, charming, and truly Western man, and I felt myself in the seventh heaven of that world that I had been trying to reach for the last few years.

We were sitting in soft leather armchairs around a small, low table, drinking fantastic coffee with whipped cream and sipping cognac from tiny glasses. The consul was charm itself!

I had had the sense not to wear my evening "working" clothes, and I looked modest and respectable: white American slacks, a dark red T-shirt of pure cotton, and a snow white Puma-brand jacket. Very light makeup, slightly toned glasses, and a red Adidas purse.

"What a shame that you do not speak Swedish," the

consul said sincerely, turning to me. "But that can be fixed, it can."

His Russian was as good as mine. When he switched to Swedish to talk with Edik, his eyes, kindly and attentive, turned to me. As if he wanted to be sure that I didn't understand Swedish.

I smiled and looked questioningly at Edik. But Edik was in no rush to translate. And, months later when I learned what was said, I understood why. The consul, still smiling at me, said the following:

"I don't have the right not to give you the document confirming that you are not married and are of sound mind, which the Russian authorities justly require in order to register a wedding between a foreigner and their citizen. My secretary is taking care of it."

"Thank you," Edik said with a smile.

"Even though I have my doubts about the soundness of your mind."

"Why is that?" Edik chuckled.

The consul warmed up my cup of coffee graciously and personally put in the whipped cream. And went on in Swedish.

"Because, Mr. Larsson, you are planning to marry a professional prostitute, which is obvious to the naked eye. Don't even try to argue. I have long and sad experience in this line. I've handed out hundreds of these affidavits."

"I don't give a damn what Miss Zaitseva did in Russia. I only care about what she will do when she is Mrs. Larsson in Sweden."

"I can predict that for us." The consul added cognac to my glass. "Eighty percent of similar marriages break up immediately or shortly after crossing the border. The majority of these girls take up individual prostitution, work in a strip bar or sex show, or end up in the brothels of Europe. Do you have any guarantee that you and Miss Zaitseva will end up among the twenty percent of happy marriages?"

"It all depends on me, Mr. Consul."

"I doubt it." The consul lit a cigarette and said to me in Russian, "Please forgive us, Madam. Be bored just another few minutes. Formalities. . . ."

And switched back to Swedish. "Think about it, Mr. Larsson, should we fill our small country with the rejects of Russian society? Don't we have enough problems of our own? I am speaking to you now as an official representative of Sweden in the USSR."

I swear I could sense that something was going on! I didn't understand for shit, and Edik and the consul behaved so sweetly and innocently, that there was no reason to be suspicious. But for some reason, my mood was spoiled.

Edik got up and said in Russian, "Mr. Consul, I was happy to introduce you to my future wife. Now I would like to receive the document and not hold you up any more."

"I think the document is ready," the consul said in Russian. He smiled at me and pushed a button on his desk.

The door opened and the consul's secretary, a skinny crone in gold-framed glasses, brought in our first piece of paperwork.

. . . When Edik and I were out on the street, he took me by the shoulders, turned me to him, and asked, looking right in my eyes, "Do you love me, Tanya?"

This question was extremely important for him just then. Absolutely necessary. And I replied, almost honestly, "Of course, Edik. I love you a lot."

He took off his glasses, wiped them with a special cloth, and put them back on. And he said, "Then everything's okay. Then there's nothing to worry about."

At the Wedding Palace a woman of thirty-five or so—all dolled up in hard-to-get velvet and gold rings from Yerevan—pinned the paper from the consulate to our application, gave us our passports back, and said, without looking at me, "There's a three-month waiting period."

"Why?" Edik asked.

"So that you can be sure of your feelings."

I knew this from the list the girls gave me and so I didn't make a fuss, but Edik was very surprised. "So long?"

The broad didn't respond to Edik, she talked to me. Even though I had been as quiet as a fish, and hadn't asked about anything.

"In the Soviet Union the rules apply to everyone," she said, giving me a nasty look with her poorly made up eyes.

Right. Mr. Larsson was a foreigner, I was one of our own. So why stand on ceremony with me?

"Thank you," I said meekly. "Good-bye."

○

In his hotel bathroom I took off the black lace stockings and the lace garter belt, folded them neatly, and put them away in my makeup bag. You're not going to wear all that in the summer heat. You only bring that for work. Many of the clients prefer it. It's their money. Every porno flick and magazine flaunts them.

41

I took a quick shower, dried off with the shaggy towel, put on my panties, corduroy jeans, and shirt, and quickly made up my face.

As I put the makeup back, I saw Edward's shaving brush stiff with soap suds again. I rinsed it, put it on the shelf, and cried out, "Edik! You haven't even taken your stuff out of the bathroom!"

"I know. In a minute."

The room wasn't made up. The bed was a shambles. His yellow leather suitcases and bags were packed. A duffel bag lay on the bed.

Edik was at the coffee table in his underwear. He had different types of money, documents, and papers spread out before him. He was adding up his Leningrad expenses on a calculator and writing them down in his notebook.

"Edik! Hurry it up!" I begged.

"Almost done!" Edward folded up the money and documents into his wallet, put the calculator in its elegant case, and put everything into the pockets of his jacket, draped on the chair back. Just a minute, Tanya."

And he went into the bathroom. I sat down and called my mother.

"Ma! It's me. Set the table, we'll be there soon."

"Are you crazy!" Mama shouted. "You could bowl in here, it's so empty. Give me a couple of hours, I'll have time to run to the market."

"Mama! You know the old joke, 'Zhora, fry some fish.' 'Where's the fish?' 'Don't worry, start frying, there'll be fish.' That's the situation, don't worry, there'll be fish. We'll bring everything. Get Lyalya to help you clean up. Send her out for bread and coffee."

"But why the rush? Why does it have to be in the afternoon?"

"Because the show has closed and they're leaving by car tomorrow at five in the morning, and Edik needs to get some sleep for the road."

"By car? All the way to Stockholm?"

"If you can imagine that. Ciao!"

○

We came out of the elevator into the crowded lower lobby. Edik with the duffel bag in his hand, me without packages. It was lunchtime and very busy. Tourists were coming back from museums, porters were hauling baggage, the Intourist guides were all over the place, and black marketeers were lurking and working.

I bowed to Tolya and Zhenya—our "specials"—from afar. Edik asked Petr Nikanorovich, the doorman, to get a taxi. The retired man hurried out, stopped a cab, and ran back to us with a bow. Edik gave him a dollar, and Petr Nikanorovich saluted, like a raw recruit. We got in the taxi and drove off . . .

○

We had to stop in front of number 32 again. That huge Sovtransauto truck was blocking the way.

Edik paid up, we got out, and walked.

"Volvos are very good cars," Edik said proudly. "We sell a lot of those cars to you. The highway from the Stockholm port on Malmo passes our house; they're always on it."

I took his arm gratefully, looked at the Volvo truck, and for some reason, took note of the license plate—ABE 51–15.

"It's wonderful that there is such close cooperation between our countries." I tried to keep in step with his long stride. "Let's you and I have a small economic agreement."

"Fine. We should have everything clear between us."

"Beautiful. Listen . . . A few days ago I bought a fur coat for my mother. For the winter. I would like it to be a present from you. As if you bought it."

"But that wouldn't be true. That's not good," Edik said, worried.

"All right, all right. It would be much worse if I did it. Mama would have a lot of unnecessary questions."

"But we don't give winter presents in summer."

"You don't. But we prepare our sleds in the summer. That's our little national quirk. So, can you help me out?"

Edik shrugged uncertainly. And we reached our lobby.

○

I must say that Mama's first international party went off well.

Everything was tasty, nothing was overdone, Mama looked wonderful, and was now sitting opposite Edik and listening with exaggerated interest to everything that I already knew by heart from the expo brochures.

"Belitronics manufactures robotics. And recently we started a series of robots for automatic fishing. I worked in the development of the robot . . ."

"You don't say?" Mama asked socially.

Lyalya and I were smoking in the kitchen.

"Yes. It weighs only fifteen kilos. The robot throws the line and pulls it in. When the fish nibbles, the robot automatically calculates. If the fish is big and strong— it can be over forty kilos—the robot leads it around, tires it out, and then quickly pulls it on board."

"Girls! Did you hear that? It's amazing!"

I could see from Mama's eyes that she didn't understand a thing about those stupid robots and was exhausted from the strain.

"Time for the show," I whispered to Lyalya. "Do you know the routine?"

"Yes."

"Go to her. Hold her there, so that she doesn't stick her nose in here. Edik!" I called. "Can you come in for a second?"

"Excuse me," Edik said with a bow to my mother and came into the kitchen. I handed him the package with the fur coat and gave him a kiss for boldness. "Do it!"

Edik came into the room bearing the package.

"Dear Alla . ."

"Sergeyevna," I helped him quietly.

"I know," he hissed. "Dear Alla Sergeyevna. Since you are the mama of my bride Tanya, I want to give you a small present from me."

"Ah, you shouldn't have, Edward." Mama was embarrassed and even stood up from the table."

"Please." Edik handed her the package.

"Thank you. I am very grateful. But really, you didn't have to . . ."

"Oh, what is it?" Lyalya squealed in a phony voice.

"Why don't you help her open it and see?" I said, jumpily.

Lyalya instantly tore open the package, pulled out the polar fox, shook it, and put it over Mama's shoulders.

Mama was about to faint. Lyalya squealed with delight almost naturally.

"Thank you, Edik." I kissed him again.

He really saved me! But then I looked at him and saw that he was stunned too. I got worried about him.

"A nightmare," he whispered. "I didn't know it was such an expensive gift. I thought . . ."

"Shut up," I said without moving my lips. Then I shouted at my mother, "Mama! If you only knew how great it looks! How did Edik guess that you needed a fur coat . . . Oh, Edik, you're wonderful!"

And my mother, my skinny mother, stood there in the luxurious Norwegian fox coat—the first fur coat in her whole forty-eight years—and stared at me. Then she sighed convulsively and said sadly, "You're crazy. You're all crazy."

A month later I was coming out of the Torzhkovsky Market with two huge bags and making my way slowly to the taxi stand, when a Mercedes pulled right in front of me and Zina Meleiko in full war paint jumped out.

"Where've you been, Tanya?"

"Hi, Zina," I said and saw that she'd already been drinking. "Isn't it a little early in the day?"

"Not to worry, Tan. S'fine. I can do anything I want now."

"Who'd you buy?" I asked. I looked in the car. The driver was a typical John—an Italian of fifty or so. Gray-haired, handsome, and obviously loaded.

"I've been bought for ten days a hundred fifty per. Not bad, eh? Ten days—fifteen hundred greenbacks."

"Good for you!" I was sincerely pleased for her. "What a deal! But what about the 'specials?' "

"The amazing thing is that they're out of the picture. They pick up everybody, but not me. It kind of hurts my feelings," Zina said with a laugh.

"Someone on high must have twisted their tails."

"That's what I think. The client has some defense contracts with our Navy for about seventy million! And they must have told our vice boys to sit quietly. For that much money they'll let the guy screw every hooker in Leningrad rather than lose the contract. That's political economics for you, Tanya."

"Maybe they'll even give you a medal," I joked.

"That's for sure. They'll catch up with me and give it to me."

The Italian got out of the car, bowed to me, and said something in his lingo to Zina.

"He wants to know if you need a ride."

"No, thanks."

Zina explained in Italian (she's got the lingo down pat) and said to me, "Listen, Tanya . . . I wanted to warn you about something. . . . You've already applied to the Wedding Palace?"

"A month ago . ."

"Now, here's what I've heard." Zina looked around. "I don't know if it's true, but just in case. You've got to spend the next two months until you get married, while he's in Sweden, writing and getting lots of letters. All full of love! You have to! And call him as much as possible—don't be cheap. This will prove that the marriage is for real. That it's not just that you want to live abroad, but you're getting married for wild passionate love. Get it?"

"Got it. Do you think that they read the mail and bug the phones?" I'd heard something like that before.

"I don't think anything and I don't know anything. And I didn't tell you anything. It may all be wrong. But what if it's not?"

"Thanks. Why aren't you doing it?" I nodded toward the John in the Mercedes.

"Who'd let me out? Have you forgotten I did a full sentence under Article 88? And then my mother in Pskov is sick, my father is on disability. My daughter lives with them, she'll be graduating next year. How can I go?"

"You have a daughter that age?" I was stunned. "God, I had no idea."

"Well, I do," Zina said so sadly. "I'm just about to hit forty. I just try to look my best, but who's going to want me when I'm pushing fifty?"

"Cut it out, you're fine."

"Yes! And another thing, Tanya. Do you have any money?"

"About seven hundred."

"Leave yourself a pair for living expenses, and put five in an account in your mother's name. And hide the book. When you leave, at least she'll have some dough. Then you can call her from there and say, surprise! Keep quiet about it now. Isn't that a good idea? OK! Ciao, Tanya!"

"Thanks, Zina. Thanks, my dear," I said and watched, as the beautiful sexy lady (who looked twenty-eight, thirty tops) walked to the golden brown Mercedes, and her client waved to me and smiled with all one hundred of his porcelain teeth.

I waved to him and headed for the taxi stand with my shopping bags. And there was a line for an hour there, at least!

49

○

I didn't learn about what happened at my mother's school that day for a long time. She told me about it much later.

Mama was having a class in her seventh grade, and one of the kids was being a real pain. He had a small TV set under his desk and was watching it. Naturally, everyone around him was trying to see the screen too.

"Yuri Kozlov!" Mama said. "You're bothering me. Leave the room."

"I won't," Kozlov replied calmly.

"Way to go!" The boys supported him and the girls watched my mother with avid interest.

"You're bothering me," she repeated helplessly.

"And you're bothering me."

"Then I'll leave!" Mother's lips were trembling.

"Go ahead," Kozlov sneered. "Who's stopping you?"

To keep from bursting into tears, Mama ran out of the room. She ran down the empty hallways to the principal's office and flung open the door. The principal, a young man of thirty, looked at the clock, at Mama, and lifted his brows: What's the problem? Why are you here before the bell?

"Albert Ivanovich," Mama said in a trembling voice. "This can't go on like this . . . Kozlov is breaking up class after class. He's so rude, Albert Ivanovich! It's a nightmare . . ."

"I'm glad you're here, Alla Sergeyevna. I was about to send for you."

"Something has to be done, Albert Ivanovich. I'm begging you . . ."

"We received a warning, Alla Sergeyevna." The principal didn't even ask her to sit down. "Your daughter is marrying a foreigner and planning to leave the Homeland? This brings us to unpleasant thoughts. How can we entrust the education of children to you, if you couldn't bring up your own daughter in the spirit of loyalty to the state that fed and clothed her."

"Oh my God!" Mama was distraught. "She's in love! And she's not going to change her citizenship. She was, is, and will be a Soviet!"

"I don't know, I don't know."

"But the times are different now, Albert Ivanovich!"

"For you and me, people who are entrusted with the formation of a child's personality, Alla Sergeyevna, the times must always be the same." Just then the bell rang in the corridor.

"How terrible," Mama said.

Now I study Swedish when I'm on duty. Of course, at night and when there are no emergencies in my department. I got a few books and dictionaries. I spread them out, study words, which I copy out into a notebook, and repeat in a whisper, and translate slowly.

Lyalya sits next to me. She's studying for her entrance exams. Not far, on the couch, the old woman Sergeyevna naps.

Lyalya yawns and slams shut her textbook. "I'm too groggy to understand a thing."

"Study, silly," I say. "If you don't get in this year . . . Study. I'm studying."

"If I had your goal . . ." Lyalya stretches.

"Stop fooling around."

We heard the phone ring in the orderlies' room. Our doctor on duty, Klavdiya Mikhailovna, came out and waved to me. I walked over.

"Your mother," she said.

I got scared—it was one-thirty in the morning! I rushed into the room and grabbed the phone. "What's the matter with you, Ma?"

"Tanya, forgive me for bothering you. Edik called from Stockholm and said that he'll be on the evening flight tomorrow. He got an individual tour for ten days and now he'll be in time for the wedding."

"Damn it, you scared me! He's coming and the hell with him! Are you all right?"

"Yes," Mama said and started to cry.

"Mama! What's the matter? Do you want me to come right home?"

"No, no, I'm just a little tired. And I wanted to hear your voice."

"What's happening, Mama?"

"Nothing. . . . Just some nonsense at work. That Kozlov is driving me crazy. I've told you about him. He's always rude and nasty . . . horrible boy. His parents are very nice, but the child is hellish. I can't wait for the school term to end."

"Don't get upset, Mama. Just a week to go. Calm down, dearest. Take forty drops of Korvalol and take a Relannum tablet. And tomorrow we'll go meet Edik's plane. All right?"

"Forgive me, Tanya. I keep burdening you with things."

"Don't worry, Ma. Will you find the Korvalol?"

○

Toward morning groans and cries came from the women's ward.

"Oh God! Help me! Oh, girl . . . I can't take it!"

And there was so much deathly depression in that voice that it scared me. I ran to the room, looked into the open door, just as Klavdiya Mikhailovna came running out.

"Tanya! That old lady, Petrokanskaya, did she get her pain shot last night?"

"It's not my ward, Klavdiya Mikhailovna . . ."

"Give her a shot immediately! Where's Nina? Damn you all to hell!"

I ran to Nina's post. The earth had swallowed her up. I ran to the nurse's station. I saw that the fool was putting the syringes into the sterilizer for the morning shots. I wanted to choke her!

"Nina! Did you give Petrokanskaya from Ward 3 a pain killer?"

"Of course! Everything's in order."

"What did you give her?"

Nina ran to the door, shut it tight, and said softly, "Tanya, what difference does it make what you give her? She's going to kick the bucket any day now."

I'll kill her, I thought. But I controlled myself. I asked very softly, "And you sell the drugs that are intended for the old woman, you bitch, is that it? Where are the ampoules?"

"Tanya . . ."

"Where's the morphine ampoules, you lousy shit?"

"Here." Nina dug under her white coat and took two ampoules out of her pocket.

I tore them from her hands, got a syringe and needles out of the boiling sterilizer, and as I ran through the door, I said, "You should be working in the morgue, you shit!"

О

That morning I came out of the bank, opened up the brand new bankbook and check: number so-and-so, account so-and-so, in the name of Zaitseva, Alla Sergeyevna, deposit 5,000 rubles, a scrawled signature. . . .

I put the book in my purse and headed for mother's school.

"Come 'ere, you," I said to him when I found him and his gang behind the school.

They were smoking openly and talking in coarse put-on tough guy voices.

"Yuri Petrovich to you," he said and looked me over, the son of a bitch, like a grown up man. It made me uncomfortable.

I had just wanted to talk to him. I thought that he was closer in age to me than to my mother and so we would be able to talk like peers. I thought I would tell him and he would understand.

"All right, Yuri Petrovich. We need to talk."

"That'll be a quarter," he said, snickering, and his whole gang roared with laughter.

I had heard that so many times! And exactly in that tone of voice. From the restaurant maitre d's who put us next to foreigners, from the floor ladies, from "trawlers," the cabbies who always work with prostitutes. And from all kinds of scum! And I paid. I had to pay them. But now . . . When that fourteen-year-old bastard was talking to me like that!

"Fine," I said calmly and took out a twenty-five ruble note. "Come here."

He walked over with a hood's rolling gait.

I gently put my hand on his shoulder, spat a juicy

wad on the note, and smacked it on his forehead as hard as I could.

He fell back, hit the wall, and landed on a pile of bricks.

"Don't move!" I barked at his gang. "Just try moving a finger!"

Without taking his stunned and angry eyes from me, the kid felt around for a brick.

I came over, stepped on his hand, and said, "You lousy little shit, you creep, you jerk and asshole, if you ever give Alla Sergeyevna Zaitseva, your teacher, the least bit of grief or say even a word in her class again I'll smear you all over the wall. Get it, shithead?"

I pressed my heel into his hand and took out a Dunhill cigarette and a lighter from my purse. I lit up and said, "I don't hear you."

Grimacing in pain, he said, "I get it."

"Good boy." I turned to his pals. "That holds for all of you. So long, children."

And I left. I didn't hear a single word from them.

I was reciting a once-beloved poem and stopped.

"Why are you peeking, Tanya? Just ten years ago you knew this whole early cycle by heart." That was Mama's way of bragging about me to Edik.

"Ah, the good old days," I chuckled and shut the book.

We were in the rooftop restaurant of the Evropeiskaya Hotel, where Edik had invited Mama and me for a dinner "for the family." The table was set for a major feast. There was a bouquet of red roses in a crystal thingamajig. Among the caviar, sturgeon, and pate lay our wedding pictures and three books that Edik had brought for Mama from Sweden.

"Edik, you're wonderful!" Mama had had some champagne and was chattering nonstop. "How did you ever think of it?"

"I didn't," Edik said honestly. "I asked a Russian in

Stockholm, 'What can I bring from Sweden to Russia for an intelligent middle-aged lady?' He said, 'Pasternak, Vysotsky, Tsvetaeyva.' I went and bought them."

"Just like that? Went and bought them?" Mama was amazed.

"Yes."

I'd only been to the Evropeiskaya twice. Not my turf. Who wants to be called into the ladies room and have your face bashed in by your colleagues for treaty violations?

Once I got the feeling that the waiter knew me. His face was totally unfamiliar to me, however. He even winked at me and nodded his head toward Edik. Then I got it: that bitch wanted me to pay him off in valuta!

"Did you want to say something?" I asked and stared him down.

"No, no! Sorry . . ." He got scared and scurried off.

A minute later Lyosha Chumakov, a detective from the local vice squad, showed up as if by accident in the half-empty daytime restaurant. He looked around disdainfully and left.

"Let's drink to our Mama, Edik!" I proposed.

"Right. If I may, I will call you Mama, now." Edik raised his glass.

"Of course, of course!" Mother was darling! I hadn't seen her like that in a hundred years. "You know, Edik, the last time I was in a restaurant was almost twenty years ago."

"Why?" Edik asked.

Mama shrugged in confusion.

I kept sipping the champagne, which I hate, and pictured (quite accurately it turned out) the scene downstairs in the vice room of the Evropeiskaya.

○

Chumakov picked up the phone and dialed "my" "specials," at the Intourist.

"Tolya? Hi. This is the Evropeiskaya. Chumakov."

"Hello, Lyosha."

"Tolya, you recently mentioned that your Tatyana Zaitseva hasn't shown up for three months now. That she had given it up . . ."

"Well?"

"Well, she's upstairs in our restaurant right now. With a businessman and some old broad. Flowers on the table, champagne . . ."

"Is the businessman yours?"

"Yes. We checked. Edward Larsson. Sweden. Individual tour."

"I know him. He was with us for the expo. And the broad is skinny, around fifty?"

"Yes."

"No problem. That's her mother. Zaitseva . . . Wait, I'll check." Tolya went into his Talmud, found me, and went on, "Zaitseva, Alla Sergeyevna. Teacher of Russian and literature. Is totally and blissfully unaware of her daughter's primary profession."

"Has Tanya moved over to our hotel to work? We've got more than enough of our own."

"No. Don't be afraid. She got married yesterday. Now she's Mrs. Larsson."

"Where's the guarantee?"

"You're right. But nevertheless . . ."

Meanwhile Edik used his pocket calculator to check the bill and the waiter stood next to him staring at the ceiling with his lying stoolie eyes and Mama and I

59

looked at the big color photos from the Wedding Palace.

"Lyalya is so beautiful!" Mama exclaimed with feigned heartiness, embarrassed like any Russian that Edik was checking the bill for a second time.

"How about Sima?" I asked.

"Sima is also good-looking. And so are Nina and Zina Meleiko. . . . But I don't look like myself at all in this one."

"It's too bad that Konstantin Ivanovich got blotto."

"Tanya! You know Lyalya's papa. You should have kept an eye on him. God! You look so good in white! And the veil . . . And Edik in a real tuxedo! . . . Marvelous!"

I was a little tired of mother's exclamations and took the list I got from Kisulya and Gulliver from my purse, looked at it, and told Edik, who was carefully counting the change, "Now we have to go to your consulate and have our marriage certificate notarized and you have to write a formal invitation for me to come to Sweden."

○

As opposed to our first visit, the General Consul of Sweden was cool and reserved. No coffee, no whipped cream, nothing.

He barely glanced at me, bowed curtly to Edik, and said, "My secretary will take care of you. Please excuse me. Business."

Edik wasn't particularly friendly either. But I turned to the consul, smiled as charmingly as I could, gathered my wits, and said in Swedish, "You are very kind, Mister Consul. We are very grateful to you."

My newly acquired Swedish phrases created a sensation: the consul arched his brows in surprise, Edik almost fainted, and the old Swedish witch in wire-rim glasses stared at me like I was the seventh wonder of the world.

"Congratulations," the consul said sourly with a bow. "You are very talented. I think that Mr. Larsson is unbelievably lucky. As, naturally, I hope you will be, too, Mrs. Larsson."

A few days before our flight Edik took me to the circus. We went down to the Evropeiskaya lobby and Edik left me by the souvenir kiosk while he went to the Intourist service bureau for tickets.

Not far from me I heard very fluent but heavily accented English. I looked and saw a very drunk John being worked on by two flashily dressed Intergirls.

And I heard one of them say, "Just a moment," and come over to me.

"Hi, Tanya."

"Hi, doll," I said. "Who are you?"

"I'm Liza the Bunny. Heard of me?"

"Of course. Greetings!"

"Tanya," said the Bunny. "We know you and respect you. But our girls asked me to tell you that you shouldn't come here any more. Let everyone have her own garden. Otherwise. . . . Why do you want any hassle?"

Edik came over with the tickets for the circus.

"Bunny, I'd like you to meet my husband, Edward Larsson. Tell the girls that I'm out of circulation and not invading their turf. Ciao."

"Good luck," Bunny said, calmed down.

When we got out on the street, Edik said "What a strange name, Bunny."

"That's not her name. It's her nickname."

He looked puzzled.

"I'll explain later. Let's go, we'll be late."

O

In the intermission, while they set up the lion cage, I went out for a smoke and Edik lined up for ice cream.

The circus was packed with foreigners. It seemed as if Intourist had bought up all the seats from the first row to the balcony. You could hear Polish, and French, and German, and English.

"Hello, Tanya-san. How do you do? I'm very glad to see you."

I turned, and there was this nice-looking Japanese man of fifty or so. I couldn't remember his name to save my life. I did remember that he was my client for a whole week during last year's fur auction. And I remembered that he didn't know Russian. And paid through the nose. Like all the Japs.

"I saw you here with a man," he said in English. "And I didn't want to disturb you. But when you are free, tomorrow or the next day, please call me at the Astoria. Do you remember the hours of the auction?"

"Yes," I said. "Quite well."

"The rest of the time I will be free for you."

And he gave me his business card, where he had written in his phone number at the Astoria. And he bowed and bowed.

I could see Edik coming toward us with the ice cream. I didn't have time to tell the Jap that I was no longer in the business that interested him. Like a fool, I stuffed his card into my jacket pocket and said hurriedly, "All right, all right . . . Excuse me, please."

The man had also seen Edik and said in farewell, "I've spent the whole year thinking about the days we spent together. I'll be waiting." And he vanished in the crowd.

No sooner had Edik and I started on the ice cream than the bell rang. Everyone started heading back inside. I held back in the hallway and threw the business card away along with my cigarette . . . The hell with him.

I took Edik by the arm and devouring our ice cream we went in to watch the lions.

○

The next day I went on my twenty-four hour duty. The normal hospital routine began in the morning: shots, rebinding wounds, IVs, pills . . .

"Tanya! Boris Semyonovich wants you!"

I dropped everything and ran to the department chief. Our young doctor, Vladimir Alexandrovich, was sitting on the windowsill of his office.

"Hello, Boris Semyonovich!"

Boris Semyonovich is a sweet, witty man and a doctor by the grace of God. A terrible coward! He'd turn in his grandmother out of fear.

"What are you doing to me, Tanya? This is awful!

How can I write a reference for someone leaving the country for good?"

"Boris Semyonovich, dear man! Why are you so worried about it? Write whatever you want," I said to calm him down. "You know it's just a stupid formality."

"Don't drive me crazy! I have to take on a serious political responsibility and you just . . ."

"Wait a minute, Boris Semyonovich," Volodya said. "What do they want from you? The truth. So you write the truth about Tatyana Nikolayevna. And I, as union organizer of the department, will sign it. If it's the truth."

"And I'll dictate it," I added. " 'Tatyana Nikolayevna Zaitseva does not smoke, pop pills, or shoot up. She drinks with revulsion, only to be polite, in accordance with all the rules and regulations. She is for peace and friendship of nations. Her motto is Proletariat of the World, Unite! She is politically literate and morally stable.' Well, will that do?"

"Terrific!" Vladimir Alexandrovich said.

"Don't you dare turn this into a joke!" shouted Boris Semyonovich. "You two are young idiots! I'm old and I don't belong to the party."

"Boris Semyonovich, this is getting boring." Volodya got down from the windowsill.

"I'd like to see you in my place, Volodya."

"So would I."

"All right," I said, getting angry. "I'm missing something here. Boris Semyonovich, are you giving me a reference for the visa people or not?"

Boris Semyonovich clutched his bald head tragically. "If you write a good one, they'll say, what were you thinking about? You didn't work closely enough with your people if you didn't realize she was going to leave. If you write a bad one, they'll say, why the hell did you keep her on so long?"

"That's it!" I said. "Gotta go. I've got work to do."

○

In the afternoon I was "walking" a nice girl after her operation. She had her arm around my shoulders, I had her by the waist, and we shuffled along the corridor together.

"Don't hold on to your belly, the stitches won't break. Step lively!"

"But what if . . ." she whined.

"Do you want to have adhesions? Why didn't you walk yesterday?"

"I was waiting for you. I'm not afraid when I'm with you."

"Silly! Move, move . . . Do you have children?"

"Two. Four and eighteen months."

"Who's with them now? Your husband?"

"My mother came from Kharkov."

"Typical man. They all know how to make babies. But when it comes to . . ."

"No, no, Tanya, he's very busy. His job. Enough, Tanya, I can't walk anymore."

"Lena, you must. Just one more time down the hall . . . Come on!"

"Oh!" Lena cried. "Tolya! It's my husband."

I looked down the corridor and saw the senior operative of my "special" vice squad, Captain Anatoly Andreyevich Kudryavstev.

He was wearing his suit and a tie, his "pop" glasses,

a white lab coat, and carrying a plastic bag. Flowers peeping out of it.

"This is interesting," I said. "Is that your husband?"

"Tolya!" Lena rushed toward him. "Oh, Tanya! Hold me."

Tolya ran over and grabbed Lena from the other side.

"Tolya, I'd like you to meet Tanya," Lena said, hugging her husband. "She sat up the whole night with me after the surgery."

"Anatoly Kudryavstev," he said.

"Tatyana Zaitseva," I said. Two can play that game.

"Did you bring it?" Lena demanded.

"Of course?" Tolya took out a box of chocolates and five carnations.

"It's for you, Tanya," Lena said. "For everything!"

"Thank you," I said and asked brazenly, "Where did you get such terrific candy?"

And he replied very calmly, "In one of the Intourist hotels. At the buffet."

"Not for valuta?" I asked.

"Don't be silly," he replied with a laugh. "Where would I get it?"

○

That evening he and I stood together in the smoking area and had a cigarette.

"Have you finished the paper work?" he asked.

"Don't ask. . . . Certificates, references . . . It's enough to kill you."

"How can you leave your mother?"

"That's the hard part. If I could only take her with me."

"She won't go."

"Yes. You're right. It's a tragedy."

"You're right, there. But if you were to look more closely, you're a tragic figure, too."

"Oh, come on," I chuckled. "Look in the mirror, captain. You've been wearing that suit for over three years now. Why is that, eh?"

What a bitch I am, I thought. Why am I picking on him? Each to his own, after all. But he didn't even blink. He took a puff and said, "How am I supposed to buy one? On my two hundred ninety rubles a month? Or on Lena's one ten? A suit costs two twenty, two forty. Lena's winter boots are one sixty. Renting a dacha for the summer for the kids is four fifty or five hundred. And they have to eat three times a day, not just on major holidays. And you know I don't take money on the side."

"I know, I know," I said. "We all know all about you. So which of us is the more tragic figure, Tolya? You or me?"

I stared at him and felt that I had made my point. If he answered, I would give him another jab.

He didn't reply.

Why am I so nasty, I thought. Why did I hit him so hard? I felt like crying.

"Thank you, Tolya. And please forgive me, I was a bitch. Don't worry. Everything will be okay. Off to work?"

"Yes."

"Say hi to everyone."

"All right."

He went out, and I went back upstairs.

At the regional OVIR office, where you get exit visas, I was seen by a plump blonde with a pleasant face—a major in the militia. She was clearly over forty, but she had a lively eye, her makeup was deftly put on, and her hands were lovely and well tended.

"You're missing certain papers, without which we can't start processing you, Tatyana Nikolayevna," she said and opened my file. "Here, let's go over it together. Marriage certificate, invitation to Sweden, applications, references . . . Paper from the TB dispensary, from the psychiatric ward, from the VD clinic . . . Let's go on. Permission from your mother, Zaitseva, Alla Sergeyevna, notarized . . . fine. But where's your father's permission? Hm, Tatyana Nikolayevna?"

It was like being thrown from the tenth floor.

"What father? I lived my whole life with my mother. I never had a father."

"Tatyana Nikolayevna, do I have to explain to you that children are usually born through the participation of a man at some point? And you must give us his permission, notarized, that he has no financial claims to you and gives his parental consent for your move abroad."

"Goddamn it!" I was pissed. "But he left us over twenty years ago! My mother shouldered the whole burden. Always! We haven't had a penny from him all these years! I swear!"

"I'm quite ready to believe you. But nevertheless . . ."

"What if he's dead? Then what?"

"Your father, Nikolai Platonovich Zaitsev, is in good health and lives at . . ."

The major pulled a piece of paper from her desk and handed it to me.

"There, take it. We knew this conversation would occur and we got your father's address. Hurry, Tatyana Nikolayevna. If you delay handing in this document, a great part of the others will lose force within a certain period, and you will have to start almost from the beginning. That will hold up getting your visa and passport. If your question is decided positively, of course."

"There could be a negative decision?" I asked.

"Of course," the major said with a smile.

○

I was so furious on my way to the address that when the cab got there, I jumped out without paying.

"Hey!" the driver shouted. "How about the fare?"

I tossed him a three-ruble note, apologized, and watched him drive away. I checked the building number with what was written on my piece of paper and went to look for apartment seventy-six. I went through the first courtyard—no. The second—also no. I saw a woman come out with a baby carriage. The carriage had about fifty empty bottles, half vodka, half cheap wine. And the woman was carefully covering them up with a rag, so you couldn't see them.

"Could you tell me where apartment seventy-six is?" I asked.

"You want the Zaitsevs?"

"Yes."

"Go to the third courtyard. There's a door in the corner by the garbage bins. A few steps down, and you'll find the Zaitsevs. Are you the doctor?"

"No."

"From Social Security, then," the woman decided and pushed her carriage.

I went into the third courtyard, found the door behind the garbage bins—the air was so foul I couldn't breathe! On the stairs it was pitch black. I used my lighter to find the apartment. I almost knocked my block off! There it was. The number was chalked on the door. No door bell of course. I knocked.

This in the middle of our Hero-City! Between the Passage and the Musical Comedy Theater! The Russian Museum was across the street, the Philharmonic Hall on the side, the Evropeiskaya Hotel nearby, foreigners walking all over the place! They should have been embarrassed for them to see this! I felt like that guy in the film, who felt bad for his country. . . . The hell with this midtown.

An old man who looked like a beggar opened the

door. He was holding a half-naked baby. Two other kids behind the old man—a boy of six and a girl of nine. They weren't dressed much better.

"The light's out on the stairs again?" the old man asked in a friendly way.

"Yes," I said.

"Come in, doctor. Forgive me, but we were told you'd be by in the afternoon."

"I'm not a doctor. I need Nikolai Platonovich Zaitsev."

"Oh, you're from Social Security! I'm Zaitsev." The old man was pleased and shouted in the depths of his nightmarish apartment. "It's not the doctor, Lucy! It's a comrade from Social Security to see me!"

He handed the baby to the girl. "Larisa, take Stasik. Go into the room and play. But quietly, don't disturb your mother. I'll talk to the lady in the kitchen. Come on . . ."

I looked at them and thought, "God! This is my father! My sister, my brothers . . . How can such poverty, such bleakness exist in our day and age? It's a nightmare . . . And why is he so old? He's only three and a half years older than Mama. No. No! It's a mistake. A mistake, a mistake . . ."

"Are you really Nikolai Platonovich Zaitsev?"

"You need my passport? Just a minute, I'll get it."

He hobbled toward the bedroom, holding on to the walls.

"No, I don't. What's the matter with your legs?"

"As if you didn't know! Polyarthritis. You pay me disability. Social Security does!"

"I'm not from Social Security."

The old man stopped, turned to me, and said, "That's weird. Who are you then?"

◯

Later we sat in the kitchen, and I was afraid to even touch the table. It was so dirty, sticky, neglected.

"Why don't you get some dentures?"

"I don't have the time," he said with a smile, wiping his tears. "And I'm entitled to have them for free, as an invalid of the second group."

"And why don't you shave?"

"It's only at home that I don't. When I go to work or out, I do."

"You work?"

"Of course. Watchman at the trolley park. Every third full shift. It's very convenient. I'm lucky that I'm on disability with the right to work. So we live pretty well . . ."

"I see."

"The important thing is to get Lucy on her feet. She's been in bed since Stasik was born. The doctors say it's in her mind. How's your mother?"

"What do you care?"

"Just asking . . ."

I could hear muffled, cautious children's voices.

"My feet get so cold," my father said shyly. "Circulation is impaired by the arthritis and my feet are always cold."

"Listen," I said. "I'm getting married."

"Oh, my little girl! Congratulations."

"First of all, I'm not your little girl, and second, I need your congratulations the way a rabbit needs the clap. I'm getting married to a foreigner and moving abroad. And I need you to sign a paper at the notary's office that you have no financial claims toward me and have no objections to my leaving."

"Abroad," he said in surprise. "That's really something. So, you're leaving your Homeland? What about your mother? Did you think about her?"

"You didn't waste much time thinking about her!" I wanted to kill him.

"Oh my, oh my. We need to drink on this. Will you have a shot?"

"I don't drink."

"And that's a good thing, child. But this is my own— pure sugar, a stick of yeast, and no chemicals. When will we ever see each other again?"

I looked at him and I thought he was going to cry again.

"Damn you," I said. "Pour."

He stealthily got a murky, smeary bottle out of somewhere, two crummy penny shot glasses, and shut the kitchen door. He filled the glasses and cut an apple in half.

"Well," I said. "Let's drink, 'papa.' Let's drink to you, you son of a bitch bastard, for leaving us twenty-three years ago and never once feeling a pang: how were your former wife, Alla Sergeyevna, and your daughter, Tatyana Nikolayevna, doing? Let's drink your stinking hogwash to the fact that you've made another three kids and haven't learned how to feed them, so that maybe at the end of your useless life they will grow up to be normal children and your wife gets well!"

I drank, and he started to cry.

"Drink!" I said. "You're the one who wanted to drink. What's the difference what you're drinking to?"

He got scared and drank. He shuddered, looked up at me with tear-filled eyes, and said with trembling lips, "Why are you all so cruel?"

"When you live with wolves . . ." I said. "Get dressed. We're going to the notary."

"What for?"

"What do you mean, what for? So that you can attest that you do not object to my departure and that you have no financial claims to me!"

I saw him reach for the bottle again and covered my glass with my hand. He poured himself a shot and then smiled with his toothless mouth.

"And what if I do?" And he drank. "Financial claims."

"You have them to me?" My eyes bugged out at him. "You to me? You! Why, I'll grind you to a powder, you crummy old . . ."

"And then you won't go anywhere." He was getting more brazen with every minute. "You have to pay for everything in this life, Tatyana."

For a second I thought that this was a dream and all I had to do was open my eyes . . . He was sitting in front of me, dirty, unshaven, drunk on two lousy shots, and watching me victoriously and implacably. I gasped with revulsion and hatred, but took myself in hand and asked, almost calmly, "How much?"

"That depends," he said with a chuckle.

"How much?" I knew he had me by the throat.

He held up three dirty fingers.

"Rubles? Tens? Hundred?" I was losing control.

"Thousand," my father said and poured himself another glass.

No longer aware of what I was doing, I reached for the bottle in order to smack him between the eyes with it. He figured out exactly what I was going to do and pressed himself against the wall in horror, covering himself with his hands.

But just then the door opened and nine-year-old Larisa with little Stasik in her arms came into the kitchen and said, "Papa, help. Mama needs to make number 2. I have Stasik. Dimka's crying . . ."

That let the air out of me. I sank back into my chair, helplessly. Squinting at me, my father jumped up from the table and smiling pathetically, said, "Just a second. Otherwise, she makes in the bed and then I have to clean up, wash the sheets. Please excuse me."

"All right," I said and stood up. "I'll bring you what you ask. I'll need several days."

"Fine, fine," my father muttered, and I thought that at that second it was much more important for him to run to his wife than get the money from me. "This way, please . . ."

From the hallway, he called to the bedroom, "Lucy! Just a second! I'll just see the comrade from Social Security out!"

"Where? Where am I going to get so much money? I was shouting hysterically at Kisulya and Gulliver.

I had come to their "pad" ten minutes ago. They rented it from a traveling engineer.

The girls were unwashed, uncombed, after a long working night and a long day's sleep. The pad, like all pads used for assignations with clients was a studio apartment, almost unfurnished, with a wide, low bed, a coffee table, and a scruffy armchair. There was a mirror by the bed, a Japanese calendar with nudes on the wall. The bathroom had broken tiles and the best cosmetics in the world, and fluffy pink American toilet paper. The filthy tiny kitchen with a burner stove was filled with empty bottles of every possible kind. There were also empty cans of beer, 7-Up, Schwepps, and ginger ale . . .

And at the head of the bed, the obligatory Sharp double cassette player with a selection of the latest tapes.

"Wait, stop shouting," Kisulya said. "How much do you need?"

"Three! He wants three thou!" I screamed.

"He could ask for more, you're not the first," Gulliver said softly.

"Help me, Kisulya!" I begged.

"What's the matter, you don't have any dough?" Kisulya didn't believe me. "You worked like a horse the last year."

"How? I'm not cheap, like you. Yes, I had eleven thousand. I gave you four for the fur coat, kept two for myself, and put five in an account for my mother, so that she'll have something when I'm gone! And that's it! All I have in cash now is fifteen hundred. I can't take money from my mother's account now, and no one has an extra ruble to spare at the hospital. I need three thousand. To live to winter."

"I don't have any money," Kisulya said firmly. "I've got it all in three-percent deposits, and they don't come due for another few weeks."

"Gulliver! Sima! Scrape it up, please," I begged. "When I get over the hill, I'll pay you back, you know me."

"Tanya! I've got it all in valuta as it is, I haven't converted in a long time. One of my money changers has been arrested, I'm really worried. The second will go soon. I've only got a few 'wooden' rubles. I bought a car and had to pay four thousand extra."

"What should I do, girls? What can I do?" I was in despair.

"What are you doing, acting like a pig on a line?" Kisulya said harshly. "What are you getting at? Can't you earn it yourself? There's a show of medical equipment from all over the world, the fur buyers are here for an auction, the city is full of work, and you're playing pathetic orphan. You dog shit! Want to be purer than the rest? Now that you're married?"

"Are you crazy?" I yelled. "One little visit to the vice squad and I'll never be able to leave!"

"Who's asking you to go to the hotels? Take the key to this pad, pay us fifty a day, and work away. You're a friend, after all."

Gulliver stared at Kisulya in astonishment and said, "Girls, I'll go make some coffee in the kitchen."

And she disappeared. They had me by the throat again. Now it was my girl friends.

"So, you want fifty a day from me?" I laughed. "And you pay two hundred a month for this place?"

"Two fifty," Kisulya said. "But this is an emergency. You gotta pay in that case."

"What will I do with the hard currency? I've lost all my connections."

"I'll take it myself," Kisulya said.

"God . . . What will I tell my mother and Edik?"

"Tell them that as a model medical nurse you were called up for ten days of military training. That will almost be the truth."

At the Intourist wing of the airport Mama and Lyalya were seeing off Edik.

Lyalya was looking all over the place, while Mama was telling Edik heatedly, "If you're a medical worker, that means you have military duty. If you have military duty, then you have to go through some special training. She's had it before, but on such short notice . . . Edik! I'm very worried. Could this mean that the political situation in the world is getting worse?"

"No, Mama. Your policies are much more wisely implemented now, and the only tension left is in the East. And Tanya has nothing to do with that. We have the same thing in our country. Even the police are called into the army for a short time. Don't worry, Mama. Soon this will all be over. We will come visit you, you will come visit us . . ."

They embraced, kissed, and Mama patted him on the head.

"I love her very much," Edik said softly. "Have her call me in Stockholm as soon as she gets back."

When my husband Edward Larsson, sitting in a SAS plane, flew up into the air and dissolved in the clouds, Lyalya said dreamily, "I want to go there, too."

But Mama paid no attention to Lyalya's words. She grabbed her by the hand and turned her sharply so that she faced her.

"Where is she? Look me in the eyes instantly! Where is she, I'm asking you! Where has she been for the last three days?"

The most horrible, the most disgusting part was that I was much happier in bed with last year's Jap than with Edik. I despised myself, cursed myself with the vilest words, but I couldn't help it.

With that damned Hitiro Keneda I didn't have to put on a show with moans, sighs, and cries, which we usually use to urge on our clients and, honestly speaking, shorten the time we spend with them. Because in our profession time is very dear.

With him I didn't have to pretend.

"I've never had a woman like you."

The Japanese are generally very gentle and tender. And this one in particular . . .

Gulliver and Kisulya found him for me that very same evening, despite the fact that I couldn't remember his name. The first two days it was very hard to get back into speaking English. Then a few areas opened up in my brain, and I managed to gab acceptably.

"Tanya-san, can I give you a few presents from your Beriozka store?"

"No, Hitiro, no. I'm married now and I couldn't bring them home. Married, understand? That's why we're here, as if in a prison."

"Oh, what a marvelous prison! I'd be willing to spend the rest of my life in this prison with you!"

○

How's that poem by Kipling go? "Day, night, day, night, we march through Africa. Day, night, day, night, still through Africa . . . Nothing but dust, dust, dust from marching boots . . ."

Was he taking dope? Damned Jap!

One afternoon when Hitiro was at the fur auction and I was lying around in bed reading an old French fashion magazine, I heard two short beeps under the window. I looked out and saw Kisulya's car. I opened the door.

They had brought me some food and Gulliver reported: "Lyalya is covering for you. At home and at work. When they saw off Edik, Alla Sergeyevna put the squeeze on her at the airport. But Lyalya didn't break! A class act!"

"Hold on, Tanya," Kisulya said. "The auction ends tomorrow and . . . You're as free as the wind, married woman. Ciao! We'll come for you the day after tomorrow. Get the money ready!"

○

The next morning I peeked into the bathroom and asked Hitiro, "Coffee or tea?"

Hitiro looked at me in the mirror and smiled gently. "Good morning. Tea, if I may."

He had already finished shaving, and I noticed how carefully he washed his shaving brush. I remained in the doorway and watched how neatly he put away his shaving and washing things in his kit.

"Tea, please," Hitiro repeated, thinking that I had not understood.

"Yes, yes, of course." I shook myself out of my reverie and went to the kitchen.

Sitting at the table, already in tie and starched shirt, Hitiro drank tea with salty crackers and never took his eyes off me.

I suddenly felt embarrassed, nervously fixed my hair, and pulled Kisulya's robe tighter around me. I spoke just to say something, "Your colleagues at the Astoria must miss you. They must be nervous."

"No. They are wise and businesslike. They see me every day at the auction and know that nothing has happened to me. The five nights that I have not been at the hotel are my business. And yours, Tanya-san."

"It's all so reasonable," I said, slightly irritated.

He sensed my irritation and took my hand gently. "I have understood two things, Tanya-san. You and I will never see each other again, to my great sorrow, and you need money very much."

"You understood right."

"How much?"

"Three thousand rubles," I said grimly.

"I don't have that many rubles. How about in dollars?"

"Divide by four."

84

"Seven hundred fifty?"

"Yes."

"Do you need more?"

"No. Just seven fifty." I wanted to finish this vile conversation about money and be alone.

Hitiro silently took out his wallet, counted off seven hundred fifty greenbacks and put them on the table. Then he took out his briefcase which he brought with him to the pad from the hotel, put it on his lap, opened it, and took out a beautiful watch covered with tiny diamonds. He handed it to me.

"I'm daring to give you this watch to remember me by. It's the latest model for very rich women. The pride of Japan."

○

I didn't hear Kisulya beep outside, or open the door with her key, or hear her come in with Gulliver.

The Sharp was playing full blast and I was in a hot tub with a glass of whiskey neat in my hand, finishing off the bottle next to me.

I was really losing it by then and so when Gulliver and Kisulya appeared in the doorway fresh and perky from their tennis game, still enjoying the good weather, the together people, all I could do was raise my glass in greeting, grin stupidly, and sip in their honor.

"So . . . This is something new," Kisulya said.

"Seven hundred fifty bucks," I said, my drunken tongue fuzzy. "There . . . in the kitchen. On the table. I didn't touch it."

Gulliver pushed Kisulya aside, ran into the bathroom and grabbed the glass out of my hands. She spilled its contents into the toilet, followed by the contents of the bottle. She hauled me out of the tub. But I couldn't help her there . . .

○

"Eat, you cretin!" Gulliver shouted, stuffing an omelette under my nose. "Eat, you idiot!" You alcoholic! Drink that coffee immediately. I can't believe it. First you're like a virgin who refuses a single drink, then you tank up like a wino. Eat!"

Kisulya sat in the kitchen across the table, in the chair where Hitiro Keneda had had his tea and crackers that morning. Kisulya had dollars and rubles, a calculator, a ballpoint pen, and a piece of paper.

"You have to eat something," Kisulya said and picked up a pencil.

I sat at the table, wrapped in a big towel, and I was shaking. Gulliver almost forced a piece of omelette into my mouth, and I felt sick. I moaned, swayed, and rose from the table. Gulliver helped me to the toilet. I threw up.

"Good!" Kisulya shouted from the kitchen. "That's good. And then wash her face with cold water."

When I was back to normal and I could think and move, Kisulya pushed a pile of Soviet money at me and said, "Take your dough, it's exactly two thousand."

"What?"

"Two thousand rubles. Look." She showed me the piece of paper. "Seven hundred fifty greenbacks times three makes two thousand two hundred fifty? Minus two fifty for the pad. That leaves exactly two thousand."

"But why are you giving me three to the dollar instead of the usual four?"

"If you don't like it, go find a money changer."

Gulliver looked out the window, smoking, blowing the smoke onto the street.

"But I need three thousand," I said in confusion.

"You said yourself that you had fifteen hundred at home. Take a thousand out of your own. That'll make three," Kisulya suggested.

"This is really nice. Why are you treating me so badly, Kisulya?"

"You want me to give you four for it and then sell it for four? That's a joke. You're going to swim cross-eyed in the tub while I stick my neck out for you?"

"But aren't we friends, Kisulya?"

"The state isn't your enemy, either, Tanya. When they raise prices because the workers 'desire' it, you don't argue, do you? You don't start haggling with them?"

"Don't argue, girls," Gulliver said. "A mess is a mess. When there are six different units in the monetary system in one country, it's hell. I think that's the cause of everything."

"What six units?" I asked.

"Count them yourself! Rubles that you get at work is one; two are the checks from Vneshtorgbank, what used to be called certificates; three is the exchange ruble for dealing with socialist countries; four the exchange ruble for capitalist countries; five are the D series checks for the Beriozka stores; and six are the bonuses seamen serving abroad get! And that's not a mess?"

"What do I have to do with it, girls?"

"You're a member of that system," Kisulya argued, flicked her lighter and burned the paper with her calculations. "Well, are you taking the dough?"

"Do I have a choice?"

"Right," Kisulya praised me. "Now, girls, we have to think through every detail of Operation Pop at the Notary. So that he doesn't trick Tanya. Here's my plan . . ."

○

As the taxi brought my father and me to the notary public, I could see from afar that Gulliver was pacing impatiently in front of Kisulya's car.

"Hurry it up!" she shouted at me. "We've already had to let two people get in ahead of us!"

She pulled my father out of the taxi. "Come on, pops, move those feet!"

For a second I felt terribly sorry for him, but he whispered fearfully, "The money . . . First the money." And I stopped feeling sorry for him.

I shoved the envelope with three thousand rubles at him and dragged him to the door.

"I should count it," he said, gasping, and trying to look into the envelope.

"Don't worry, dad," Gulliver said angrily. "This isn't church. No one will trick you. Move those feet."

The line was incredible! Kisulya was at the head of the line right at the notary's door, waving her arms at us. "This way, Tanya! Hurry!" She shoved the papers at me. "Everything's all typed up. Move it!"

I pushed my father ahead of me into the notary's office and heard an old lady behind us wail, "How'd they get in without waiting in line?"

Two obnoxious fisherwoman voices replied, "What do you mean ahead of the line? Who went in ahead of the line? Are you completely blind, you old bat? You should be ashamed of yourself!"

When my father and I came out of the notary's office, Kisulya was wiping her windshield, and Gulliver was in the front, her long legs sticking out the front door.

"Okay?" Kisulya shouted at me.

I waved the paper with its stamp and seal.

"Get in," Gulliver said. I opened the back door. Kisulya got behind the wheel.

My father was still squashing the envelope with the money and looking at me pathetically. Then he exclaimed, with trembling lips, "Little girl!"

I said nothing in reply and got in the car.

"Take care, pops!" Gulliver shouted and slammed the door.

"Don't cough!" added the fearless Kisulya.

And we drove off. I turned and saw him open the envelope, look around warily, and start to count.

○

Digging deep into the friable, sparkling snow, the big Volvo Sovtransauto truck, number ABE 51–15, pulled up in front of house 38.

The driver, wearing a sweater and ski cap, jumped from his cab into a snow bank. He stopped for a second, listened, and looked up at our building. At our windows.

I could swear that he had turned to us. Even though our windows were sealed for the winter, the small airing panes in the kitchen and in the room were open, and surely our fine rendition of the sad, old song about Khaz-Bulat could be heard out in the street.

Everyone around the table was singing. Even Lyalya's father, who had managed to have more than his fill of cognac and was now almost out of commission. Aunt Tonya, Lyalya's mother, was singing, and so were Kisulya and Gulliver. Zina Meleiko sang beautifully in a low, hoarse contralto. My beloved mother sang with tear-filled eyes. Holding hands under the table, Lyalya and our young doctor Volodya sang. Where did they learn the words?

And I sang with them. Even though I can't carry a tune. I sang and looked out the window at our ugly nine-story and five-story buildings, at the poorly planned narrow and icy roads among them, at the pathetic, face-less new neighborhood that had become home to me.

And then I saw that Mama was weeping openly. I couldn't stand that. I took her by the hand, made her stand, and said, "Come on, Mama, help me prepare dessert."

I pulled her into our tiny kitchen, sat her down, and handed her a knife.

"Put out the Napoleon. I'll put out the other pastries and make some coffee."

"Some people might prefer tea."

"I'll make some tea, too."

We worked together. I was getting tired and what I feared most was my mother saying, "Don't leave me, child."

"Don't leave me, child," she said.

The very words I had feared!

"I'm not leaving you, Ma. I've got to leave. I have to change my surroundings, Mama. Otherwise I'll flip out. I've spent so many years . . ."

"Stay. I'll help you."

"Don't make me laugh."

Kisulya appeared in the doorway.

"Need help, girls?"

"No! Go back to the table. We'll be right out."

Kisulya left and I said, "I'm tired of living in constant lies. We hear one thing. See another. I lie, You know that I'm lying. I know that you know. But I go on lying and you go on pretending that you believe me! Which in itself is also a lie. And it's like that everywhere. In everything. I'm sick of it! And then, it's disgusting that a waiter or maitre d' should officially make twice as much as a teacher, engineer, or doctor. And then he steals from the restaurant, too! I'm sick of it! I won't have it! Enough!"

"All the more reason," my mother said. "Leaving your Homeland when it's in this condition is a sin. When Kuprin and Vertinsky came back from abroad, they always considered their immigration as a tragic mistake in their lives."

"Some comparison! Me and major stars. But if they

had had to go through the paperwork I did to get out, I doubt they would have come back."

And then I heard Lyalya shout, "Quiet! It's the phone! . . . An international call!" It was the loud, long ring for international calls. I ran into the room and grabbed the phone.

"Hello! Yes! I'm Mrs. Larsson. Yes!" I told everyone, "It's Sweden. Stockholm." And then shouted into the phone again.

"Yes, Edik! Everything's fine! I've already called the taxi! Yes! Don't worry! Flight SU 53. Everyone sends his best. And Mama kisses you! What? So do I, of course. All right! All right, I said! I understand! Kisses. I said kisses! Wait for me!"

I hung up and felt embarrassed by the brevity of the conversation with my husband. Even though he was the one who had hung up.

"Telephone calls are so expensive there! Much more than here."

The phone rang again. I picked it up.

"Hello! Yes, we did. We need two cars . . . to the airport. One minute!" I looked out the window. "Please tell the drivers to stop in front of number 32. You can't get to our building. There's a truck blocking the way. All right! We're waiting."

I took Lyalya into the bathroom and gave her the bankbook.

"Tomorrow, when Mama is feeling better, give her this, please. And this is for you." I handed Lyalya the diamond watch. "Only for wealthy women. The pride of Japan."

"Thank you."

"And don't be mean to Volodya. He's a terrific guy. Understand?"

"I want to go there, too." Lyalya looked away.

"Do you have to? Huh, Lyalya?" I had serious doubts.

We got to the airport just as they announced the Stockholm flight and I had to go to passport control and customs.

Mama was wearing the fox coat for the first time. There was no time for conversations and goodbyes. Volodya smoked nervously and patted Lyalya and the rest just cried like regular women.

Paying no attention to the customs agents, porters, foreigners and interpreters, Intourist and Aeroflot personnel, Gulliver, Kisulya, Zina Meleiko, and Lyalya bawled. Aunt Tonya seemed to be in mourning.

I cried and kissed my mother's hand, as if begging her forgiveness.

She looked at me in silence, dry eyed, and we both thought we would never see each other again.

In the air, as we made a final circle over Leningrad, I recognized the city, bridge-covered Neva River and said aloud to my self, "That's it. The end."

A tiny old foreigner, sitting next to me, turned and raised his eyebrows interrogatively. I sniffed and tried to smile as sociably as I could . . .

PART

II

So many times in these eighteen months in Sweden I had dreamed that one of my old friends would see me just at the moment when I came out of the Storgmarkiada—an astonishing mix of department store and supermarket.

It was an amusement park for me every time!

The big glass doors opened on their own, and I came out onto the street to my little darling Volvo 343. In my arms was the creature dearest to me in this place— Frosya, an exotic mix of fantastic blood and lineages, fuzzy and warm.

Behind me, pushing the cart filled with brightly packaged products was a fifteen-year-old boy from the store, in a uniform.

I opened the trunk of my Volvo and the boy neatly loaded my purchases into the car, all the while smiling and carrying on a sweet conversation with my Frosya.

When he was done, he slammed the trunk, handed me the keys with a bow, and thanked me for shopping at the store. At this point I tell him that he's grown a lot in the last week and looked like a real man. And I tipped him two crowns. We said goodbye and I got behind the wheel of my car.

I learned to drive and to speak Swedish rather quickly, and I had no problems with that.

Our house was twenty kilometers from Stockholm, not far from the suburban village of Salem, fifty meters from the E-4 highway, the busiest one, which leads to the south.

As is customary in small towns and suburbs, everyone knew everyone to smile at and say hello and everyone was almost always friendly.

Thus, when I drove up to our Gulf gas station in Salem, right on the highway next to our house, the attendant shouted, "Good morning, Fru Larsson!"

"Hello, Martin! Is Reya at the bar?"

"Since seven this morning. Go have your chat. I'll take care of everything and park the car by the bar."

I left the keys in the ignition, picked up Frosya, and went to the bar that was part of the gas station.

"Hi!" Reya greeted me with a smile. "Everything okay?"

"Okay! And you?"

"Yes. The usual?" She picked up a tall glass.

"Of course. And one for yourself."

"Thanks. Will you call Edward?"

"Naturally." I paid her for the call, and Reya gave me the phone and filled the tall glasses with my favorite drink, pineapple juice mixed with cream of coconut.

I dialed the Stockholm number of Belitronics.

"Hello? This is Engineer Larsson."

"Hello, Mr. Larsson," I said in Russian, and Reya listened to the unfamiliar sounds with a tense smile. "This is the Minister of the Finishing Industry of the Soviet Union, Comrade Tutkin."

"Hello, Comrade Tutkin," he replied in Russian. "I'm glad to hear your voice. What can I do for you?"

"We would like to commission specially programmed manipulators for automatic fishing of sturgeon in home conditions."

"Fine! We accept your order, Comrade Tutkin."

"In what currency would you like to be paid, Mr. Larsson? Crowns? Dollars? Rubles?"

"You see, Comrade Tutkin, unfortunately both Swedish crowns and American dollars permanently fluctuate on the world market. But Russian rubles solidly hold their constant value. That's why I pick rubles, Comrade Tutkin. Does that suit you?"

"It would suit me if you were to come home earlier, damn it! The light is out in the garage again, and I almost fell on my face when I went down to get the car!"

"Poor Comrade Tutkin! My poor little bunny! . . . Are you hanging out at Reya's again and drinking those Pina Coladas that are so expensive?"

"My health is more expensive," I said. "Edik! Hurry home. Do you know how lonely Frosya and I are?"

"All right, all right. Remember that we're having a party on Sunday?"

"I'm just back from Storgmarkiada. I've gotten everything.

"Great! Say hi to Reya. Kisses."

I hung up and raised my juice glass. "Chin-chin," Reya said, and we sipped our drinks. "I like it when you and Edward speak Russian."

"If you only knew what silly things we say."

"It doesn't matter. I like the sound of your language."

Martin came into the bar and handed me the keys to my car.

"Everything's in order, Fru Larsson. I put it on your account."

"Thank you Martin." I looked at my little car and saw a big truck pull out to the diesel pump.

Big blue letters said Sovtransauto.

I gulped down my drink. Gave Martin a tip, said goodbye to Reya, picked up Frosya, and left the bar. I wanted to get into my Volvo, but I saw the driver of the Russian truck pointing at a map and trying to find out something from Martin. The man could only shrug.

It would have been crummy not to help out the man. I went over and (bitch that I am!) couldn't resist a little playacting.

"What does this fellow want, Einar?" I asked in Swedish.

"Hello, Fru Larsson. He's trying to speak German, but the only place he could be understood is South Africa."

The Russian driver was around thirty-three, and he was handsome, the son-of-a-bitch, as if he had come off a May Day poster. He addressed me in dreadful German and showed me the map.

"All right," I said in Russian. "Don't strain yourself. What's the problem?"

He was taken aback and said anxiously, "Your Russian is so good."

"I'm a talented girl. Where're you from?"

"Leningrad. Are you local?"

"Something like that. Where in Leningrad do you live?"

"You won't know it. Science Prospect."

I grew wary. "The house?"

"What's the difference?" he said with a smile. "It's thirty-two."

I stepped back, looked at the license plates, and understood. ABE 51–15.

"So you're the bastard, damn your mother's eyes, who made it impossible for me to get to my own door? You were always spread out all over the street, as if you were the only one in the whole city!"

With Frosya in my arms I raced around the second floor of Storgmarkiada, where they sold clothes, while he hurried after me, covered with packages.

"What's your wife's hip size?"

"How am I supposed to know?" He barked at me. "Hurry it up, Tanya! You're making me feel foolish!"

"Don't be a jerk! Really, Vitya, honest, you're a fool. Why should you spend your lousy valuta, when it's not a problem for me? Come on, let's get her these tights. You can't buy tights like this from any black marketeer in Leningrad. And a pair for your daughter. That's pop! Everyone will die, it's terribly fashionable now."

○

Then we sat on the terrace of a roadside cafe, which was completely empty, and our cars—my little Volvo and his huge Volvo—were parked next to each other and regarded us with their headlights. Tired Frosya slept under the table.

"We bring plywood, Georgian wines, polyethylene, and peat," he said. "And we bring back metal powder, rear windshields with heating elements for Zhigulis from Eslov. From Klippan, seat belts, from Goteborg, spare parts for those Volvos." He pointed to his truck.

"Eat some more, Vitya," I said softly.

"You've stuffed me already!"

"How about a drop?"

"No way, Tanya! I'm driving!"

"I'll have a bit," I said and brought the gin closer.

"Oh, Tanya, you shouldn't," Vitya said, shaking his head. "The police are very strict about that."

"I'll be okay." I poured. "To you. To Leningrad . . . Your family . . . My mother."

I drank and I wanted to cry. But I didn't show it.

"When will you be back in Sweden?"

He took a company calendar out of his pocket, counted, moving his lips, and said, "If everything goes according to plan, I'll be coming down from the ferry in the Viking Line port in Stockholm on the twenty-first or twenty-second."

"Give me the calendar."

"Here.

"Thanks . . . Thank you, Vitya."

"I'm the one who owes you thanks."

"Don't be silly. Give my mother the dress and shoes we bought, and the sweater for Lyalya, and tell her that everything is very, very, very good . . ."

And I burst into tears.

At home, waiting for Edik, I started making pies. I popped in a video of American cartoons, turned off the sound, and got to work. As I rolled out the dough, I watched the TV and said to my furry companion Frosya, "Note that all these girls are from out of town! From little towns, regional centers, villages . . . They come to Moscow or Leningrad and they're normal, decent girls. They go to technical school, trade schools . . . Sorry . . ."

I poured some gin into my glass and added tonic. I took a sip and set it down.

"And it was only recently that I realized why there are so few Muscovites or Leningraders born into the business. We're quite . . . How can I put it? It's because we're relaxed to begin with. We have our parents, a roof over our heads. We don't have to fight for anything.

But they have to fend for themselves. I had to lie to my mother all the time: 'Stayed at my girlfriends,' 'Missed the last subway,' but they don't have to. If they don't come back to the dorm, who cares? I can always get some bread and butter at home, but those girls have to really scramble to eat in the big city and look good, too!"

I had some more to drink. And got back to the dough.

"They have to grab like crazy. Now notice, that everywhere, in sports, science, and business relations all the way to the very top, it's the provincials who are winning! We're yawning while they're getting the food out of our mouths. Who makes the best hard currency hookers? The most clever, the greediest, the smartest? The ones who come in on quotas. Take Kisulya. She graduated from the Institute of Culture. Gulliver was a master of sport in volleyball. When Zina Meleiko ended up in jail under Article 88, where had she been? In the final year of the university, in the philosophy department! But they're all from out of town—Pskov, Vologda, Cherepovets. . . . And in just a few years they have apartments and cars and plenty of dough. They're taking over the city!"

I raised my glass, held it up to the light, and took another sip.

"And they've got everyone on their side . . . They haul in the money and let others live well too. They pay and pay. A good valuta whore pays from fifty to two hundred rubles a day in expenses. Depending on how much she makes that day. So many birds of prey feed on us. I know from my own experience."

I tasted the dough—no salt! And none in the canister.

"Damn it! Did I forget the salt again? I've got a hole in my head. That's the second week I forgot it, can you imagine? It's a nightmare!"

I wiped my hands, took off my apron, and turned to my audience. "Sorry, Frosya. Got to go. I'll finish up when I get back."

And Frosya, my constant daily and sole audience, wagged her tail.

A twin of our house stood across the street. A mirror image. One company spread standardized well-being throughout the neighborhood.

I ran through our gate, across the street, and called to the woman watering roses under the first-floor windows. "Fru Holstrom! Fru Holstrom! I have a small request."

My neighbor turned off the water and smiled. "Whatever you need, Fru Larsson. With pleasure!"

O

Then Edik came home from work and I fed him in the living room with all sorts of things including his favorite cabbage pies. I ate almost nothing myself, just sipping my weak gin and tonic.

"Marvelous pirozniki!" Edik said. "I think I'll be made head of the department."

"Hurray!" I raised my weak drink. "I'm so happy for you!"

"It has to do with you just as much. I will get a significant raise and we will be able at last . . ."

"To buy a tour to the Soviet Union!"

"Maybe. I'd rather pay an extra mortgage payment. That would be more practical, if you look to the future."

"But we've been putting off our trip to Leningrad for a year-and-a-half." I got upset and drank almost half a glass.

"You're not fair," Edik said sadly. "If you hadn't wanted your own car last year, we could have gone to Russia. Please, don't drink anymore."

"Drink? You call this drinking? I'm sitting here sipping practically pure tonic. Here, taste it!"

"Thanks, I don't want any. Thanks, I said I don't . . . I believe you. Don't get upset. Another thing. I have a small request. Darling, don't borrow salt from Fru Holstrom any more. Don't ask her for anything. Or anyone else for that matter. Ever. I've told you several times that it's not done. Our problems are our problems and no one is required to . . ."

"That bitch!"

"I'm not finished," Edik said firmly, and I shut up for a second. "Your charming, purely Russian spontaneity can be misunderstood."

I gulped down the glass, banged it on the table, and switched to my native tongue.

"But I asked that bitch for a pinch of salt, that tightass! Has she no conscience?"

"Every nation has its national characteristics," Edik began in Russian, but he couldn't stop me. Maybe I had had too much to drink.

"That's true! Now that's true! . . You know what you can do with your national characteristics! In Leningrad it would never occur to me to wonder whether it was polite or not to borrow a pinch of salt or a piece of bread from a neighbor! Or a fiver until payday. Damn those national characteristics to hell, when everyone smiles even as they plan where best to kick you!"

"Don't be angry, dear," Edik said softly and took away the gin bottle. "Don't get upset."

That night we lay in bed each under a separate quilt. Edik read. I stared at the ceiling. Frosya wheezed next to me.

Then Edik put down his paper and turned off his light.

"What did the doctor say?" he asked.

"He said that everything seems okay to him with me. He wanted to see you."

"Oh? Strange."

"There's nothing strange about it." I put out my light. "When a man and wife want children and something's wrong, both have to be checked."

"All right, all right," he whispered and tried to put his arms around me.

Little Frosya growled at him.

"Can't you put Frosya outside?" Edik asked.

"Don't, Edik . . . I had a very difficult day today." I hugged Frosya.

Edik got up in silence, picked up his quilt, and went to sleep in the study.

Frosya and I kissed and fell asleep.

On Sunday our house looked like a foreign movie: our guests' cars parked in front, their owners and wives and children, all dressed in white or very light colors, were having aperitifs. The women were sitting in lawn chairs, while the men stood around Edik.

Edik, in apron and gloves, was at the barbecue, cooking slabs of venison, turning them with two big forks.

I was anxious about Gunwald, and I imagined the scene in his car. His behavior at the party proved how right my instincts were.

Coming up to the house, Gunwald honked at someone, and Ela looked at him in surprise. "What's the matter, Gunt? I don't understand what's worrying you?

"We're late for a party and that's impolite!"

Ela laughed calmly and gently caressed his sleeve. "My dear, it's impolite to bring your wife and children to visit a Russian prostitute."

"Ela! I beg you, cut it out. Tanya is the wife of our old friend, and you shouldn't . . ."

"Did you sleep with her, too, in Leningrad, dear?"

"Oh, God! How many times must I tell you . . ."

"And how is she in bed?" Ela lit a cigarette and looked at her husband with interest.

○

I got everything ready before the guests arrived—the barbecue, the meat, the spices, the drinks table for the adults, the dessert table for the kids, and of course, the samovar, the pride of every Swede who's been to Russia!

I knew almost all the men from the last two expos in Leningrad. I met their wives in Sweden, and now as the hostess I was knocking myself out trying to amuse their kids, over a dozen of them. From four to twelve years old.

At first I couldn't think of anything except a tug of war. Strangely enough, it was just the thing. We separated into two teams—I helped the little ones on one side, Gunwald's older son and a few others on the other side—and we began pulling, falling and tumbling, getting up and pulling again. . . .

I got so involved I didn't notice what was going on around us. Not that the heavily drunk Gunwald was staring at me, or how all the men hovered around Mr. Turrel, one of the firm's directors, or how Gunwald's wife, pregnant with their fourth child, watched our barbaric game anxiously. She was in a wicker chair eating ice cream, which she rested on her belly from time to time.

"Hey, ukhnem!" I called out, using the chant of the Volga boat men. I wanted to give the kids a rhythm.

And my little Swedes, not knowing the language, picked up the Russian "ukhnem!" and pulled each other around the whole yard with that rope. Frosya ran around us in circles, barking.

The women applauded, the men cheered us on.

It ended with the little ones straining, pulling, and getting their opponents over on their side, toppling on them. Laughter, shouts, squeals! Who won, who lost?

I climbed out from under the little bodies and saw that my dress was ruined—green grass stains all over, and a huge brown spot on my stomach.

"Horrors!"

"That's my chocolate," one of the kids explained. When we fell down, it popped out of my mouth."

"Don't worry. I'll go change, and I'll bring you another chocolate candy."

○

Upstairs in the bedroom I quickly tossed off the dress, and in my panties (I had stopped wearing bras completely in Sweden), opened the closet and got out summer jeans and a light blouse. I came across a gin bottle I had hidden away a long time ago. I picked it up— just a little on the bottom!—and finished it off.

And I heard steps on the stairs. Just what I needed, for Edik to see me drinking! I shoved the bottle under the bed and called out, "Edik, is that you?" I turned around.

Gunwald Rein, panting hard, stood in the doorway.

I grabbed the jeans to cover my top.

"What's the matter with you! Get out of here! Can't you see I'm changing?" I didn't even notice that I was speaking Russian.

Huge Gunwald blocked the door and silently, without taking his eyes off me, began unzipping his fly.

"What are you doing?" I couldn't even scream. The bedroom window was open and I could be heard in the garden. "Stop it instantly!"

I tried to squeeze past him to the door, but he grabbed me, pulled the jeans out of my hands, and showered me with kisses.

"Let me go! Let me go, you stupid drunk! Let me go!"

"I'll pay you," he muttered, pulling me to the bed. "I'll pay you more than I used to pay you in Leningrad. I hope you remember how much I paid you there?"

"Let me go, bastard! Shit! Creep!" He was twisting my arms, and I was losing strength. "How dare you! You're in my house! In my house!"

"You're in my house! In my country!" he said hoarsely, pulling down my panties. "You owe it to me that you live here. I slipped you into Edik's bed, you filth! Remember what you used to be? A prostitute!"

He threw me on the bed and feverishly pulled at his trousers. I freed my hands and accidentally found the bottle under the bed. I slammed it down hard on the head of Gunwald Rein.

The bottle shattered. Bleeding, Gunwald sank to the floor.

I jumped up, opened the bedroom door, dragged the unconscious body to the stairs—where did I get the strength?—and without any compunction shoved him down the stairs. He rolled to the bottom and lay there motionless.

. . . A minute later, dressed and combed, I was pouring mineral water on his head. The mineral water made the blood on his hair and face bubble, turning into pink foam.

When he opened his eyes the first thing he saw was the two barrels of Edik's shotgun. I swear, it was loaded and cocked.

"You bastard, zip your fly and listen to me closely," I said in a low voice. "You came into the house for some mineral water. You got dizzy. You fell and hit your head. Hear me? You hit yourself, understand? And if you say even one word otherwise, I'll shoot you. I have nothing to lose. Repeat it!"

"What?" He didn't understand.

"Repeat it, bastard: 'I went into the house for mineral water. I got dizzy. I fell down and hit my head on something. I don't remember anything else.' Well!" I aimed right at his forehead.

Without taking his eyes from the barrels, Gunwald said, "I went into the house for mineral water. I got dizzy. I fell and hit my head . . ."

"Fine. Now zip your fly and keep practicing. We'll give you first aid," I said and called out the open window. "Edik, Benny! Come here! We have a problem."

I put the shotgun behind the curtain—far from Gunwald, close to me.

A half hour later adults and children were in the yard around the samovar chatting peacefully, as if nothing had happened.

Gunwald, head bandaged and arm in sling (I think

he tore the ligaments in his elbow when he fell) was sitting grimly with a glass in his uninjured hand, and the rest were teasing him (except for Edik).

"That's not our Gunwald Rein," Benny said. "He used to be able to put away a whole cistern."

"And he never got dizzy," Stig said.

"And he certainly didn't fall down!" Kenneth went on.

Pregnant Ela Rein patted Gunwald's shoulder and smiled gratefully at me.

Edik tried to catch my eye several times, but I didn't react. Not because I was afraid of giving myself away. It's just that I was busy. The littlest Rein was on my lap and I was feeding him ice cream and making sure that he didn't get me dirty.

"Dear friends! Let's congratulate Ed Larsson with his new position and his lovely wife," said Mr. Turrel, and I had the feeling that he understood everything.

"And, Alla Sergeyevna, she asked me to tell you that things are very, very, very, very good for her!" Vitya told my mother.

She told me about this after, by phone. How Vitya had come to see her, his kind questions about her situation, his assurances about my new life, how he brought the presents for Lyalya and for her. When we spoke she didn't tell me that she had been in bed for the last ten days.

"Thank you Vitya! It's a shame that Lyalya isn't in town. She went south for a vacation. She'd be so happy!"

"Do you need anything, Alla Sergeyevna? My family is at the dacha, I'm free. Can I go to the store or the pharmacy for you? Don't hesitate to ask."

"No, no, Vitya, thank you! I have wonderful neighbors, Lyalya's parents. They're away right now, but I'm not alone. I have friends."

"Wouldn't you be better off in the hospital, Alla Sergeyevna?"

"What if Tanya calls? What if she comes with Edik?
No, I have to be home. Vitya, how does she look?"

"She has no equal. She looks great! And she's got
this car . . ."

"Yes, she wrote to me. Isn't it dangerous?"

"She's great. Drives like a pro!"

The doorbell rang. Then a key turned in the lock.
Vitya looked at Mama. "It's for me," she said with a
smile.

The door opened and in came Kozlov—that brat from
Mother's class.

He put the shopping bag on the floor, locked the
door, and put the key in his pocket. He picked up the
bag and went to the kitchen. From there he shouted,
"Alla Sergeyevna! Our drugstore doesn't have Adelgan.
I made them call the main distributor. They have it at
Tikhoretsky. I'll put away the groceries and go down
there. And I got a loaf of bread for twenty-two kopeks.
They were out of the sixteen kopek ones. The rest is
just as you had it on the list."

"Yuri!" Mother called him in. "Come here. I'd like
you meet someone."

Kozlov came in. Vitya got up and shook hands.

"Victor Evdokimov."

"Yuri Kozlov."

"Yuri is my pupil. Vitya drives long-distance trucks.
He travels all over the world." She was proud of them
both.

"Not all over," Vitya said. "Then, as we agreed, right,
Alla Sergeyevna? I load up on the nineteenth and I should

be there by the twenty-second. But you'd better mail the letter. We have strict rules . . ."

"Of course, of course! I'm so grateful to you already."

"Please get better." He said goodbye and winked at Kozlov. "See me to the door?"

When they were on the landing, Vitya took out a pack of cigarettes. He offered them to him. They lit up.

"What's the old lady got?" Vitya asked.

"Don't call her an old lady!"

"Sorry. What's the matter with Alla Sergeyevna?"

"Ischemic heart trouble. Bad pulse. Nerves. Loneliness . . ."

"How do you know all that?"

"I hear what the doctors say."

They were quiet. Then Vitya asked, "Do you need some money?"

"We'll manage."

They shook hands, and Vitya went down the stairs, while Kozlov put out his cigarette, waved away the smoke, and went back into our apartment.

Before going to work in Stockholm, Edik always had breakfast in the kitchen. I feed him and Frosya, flitting around them in a light houserobe, serving Edik coffee with cream, making toast, grating cheese, and basically rushing around like a village woman seeing her husband off into the fields. The only things missing are the pitcher of fresh milk and the crust of black bread. Plenty of everything else.

"I'd love some black bread . . ." I say longingly.

"Your people sent a telex. They're inviting us to participate in an expo. We accepted. It's very good for us."

"Hurray!" I shouted.

"I'm very happy, too. This will cut our expenses in half."

"How?"

"I'll be traveling on the company."

"Is that decided?"

"Tomorrow for sure. The chief is calling the department heads together on the twenty-third . . ."

"What do you mean? Today is the twenty-second already?"

"Of course."

I threw everything down and ran to the bathroom, yelling, "I'm coming with you! I have to be at the Viking Line port by nine!"

In the bathroom I rinsed my face and noticed the unwashed shaving brush. Irritation filled my heart. I washed it fiercely under a stream of hot water.

"Are you ever going to wash your shaving brush?"

He appeared in the doorway, rinsed his hands in the water, kissed me on the neck, and said, "What for? I could have used the same soap suds tomorrow."

O

We race down the E-4 in Stockholm in my Volvo. I was driving, Edik next to me, Frosya riding in the back on top of a small package from IKEA.

The Sovtransauto calendar was attached to the rearview mirror. The twenty-second was circled in red.

"There you see," Edik said. "One car is twice as cheap. And if you take into account that my SAAB eats one and half times as much gas . . ."

I was getting nauseated by these conversations.

"How will you get back?"

"By bus."

"Should I come pick you up?"

"Twenty kilometers here, twenty back, twenty here, twenty back. It's not worth it."

"It's not worth having a second car."

"I told you that last year."

We pulled up at Belitronics at ten to eight.

I parked the car and saw Stig, Benny, Kenneth, and Mr. Turrel, Edik's boss, drive up.

Gunwald Rein was last to arrive. He had a bandage on his head and his arm in a sling.

Kenneth, Stig, Benny, and Mr. Turrel greeted me very politely, while Gunwald tried not to look in our direction, locked his car, and headed straight for the door.

"You look wonderful, Fru Larsson," Turrel said. "Ed, as soon as you say goodbye to your wife, come to see me. Goodbye, Fru Larsson."

"Goodbye Mr. Turrel."

Five minutes later, I had kissed Edik and driven off to the intersection. I started making a left turn when an old ramshackle car drives right into the passenger door. Lucky it wasn't head on.

I blew up! My little Volvo! My favorite little car! I jumped out of the car and was so angry I didn't realize I was shouting in Russian in the middle of Stockholm.

"Damn your eyes!"

A girl my age (or a bit older) jumped out of the wreck and shouted, "Too lazy to look both ways, bitch!"

And we both shut up as we realized that we were shouting in Russian at each other.

"God," I asked, stunned. "Where are you from?"

"Moscow." The fool smiled. "And you?"

"Leningrad."

○

Then we sat in the park, smoking, and looking at our cars—mine had a dented door, hers a broken headlight.

"What are you upset about, you're lucky, someone loves you," Vera said. "I gave my jerk practically everything I made at the Intercontinental in Moscow, just so that he would marry me and bring me here. Can you imagine?"

"No."

"We came here, got divorced, he went back to Goteborg, I stayed here. And it started. I'm watched by the police—I have to pay this one and that one. And the local men pay pitifully. We foreigners are third class here. If I could get into a decent house, I'd be fine. But they don't take immigrants. The bastards! The inequality! Have you seen their whores? Skinny, ugly, but they drive around in Mercedes, the bitches. Gets me mad. I should go to Hamburg. I heard Russians are popular there again.

I listened to her and thought that I could have ended up like her, like poor Vera. We all think that the streets are lined with gold here . . .

"Of course, I have had this great offer," Vera said thoughtfully. "If it works I'll be set for life."

"What is it?" I asked, perking up.

"Well," Vera was reluctant to reveal it. "It's too early. I don't know whether I should do it or not. But if it works, then . . ."

And she knocked on the wooden bench superstitiously. And looked warily at me—was I a threat? But I'm well trained—I don't ask questions.

I looked at my watch and got up. So did Vera. I hugged the poor girl, kissed her on both cheeks, and said, "All right, Vera. I'm off. Call me. And I'll call you. And come to see me. We'll make some pies, have a shot, sing a song . . ."

"I'll call," she said hurriedly. "I'll definitely call!"

○

Frosya and I drove past the Stockholm city park, filled with colorful equestrians, with silver-haired grandpas and grannies jogging in bright running suits, and kids playing with happy morning faces, and five minutes later we were in the big square in front of the Viking Line port.

At that early hour most of the parking lot was empty, and I stopped my Volvo not very properly but in a place where Vitya could see us as soon as his wheels touched Swedish soil.

There were still thirty-five minutes for the ferry from Helsinki. Frosya came out onto the sun-warmed asphalt and sat down on a stump of some kind. And we froze in anticipation.

○

As I later learned, those thirty-five minutes were most disgusting and unpleasant ones for my husband, Edward Larsson.

"You know how I feel about you, Edward," Mr. Turrel said to my Edik in his office. "I was the one who insisted on your promotion, and I always felt you were one of the most talented engineers in our company. However yesterday at the preliminary meetings of the board doubts were expressed on the wisdom of sending you to Leningrad as our representative."

"On what reasoning?"

"Very vile. It was decided that our firm could not

be represented by a man whose wife had once led a dubious life in that same country."

"Who will head the group?" Edik asked.

"Most probably, Gunwald Rein."

"How disgusting!" Edik said and left his boss's office.

God! I didn't imagine that there could be so many cars on one ship!

That sparkling white hulk, with fifteen-foot letters spelling out "Silya Line" on the sides along with a drawing of a cartoon walrus, opened the huge gates in its nose and began spitting out so many cars that it made me gasp! It must have been a thousand.

And after them like woolly mammoths, came the heavy trucks. Several hundred. British, German, French, Polish, Soviet. . . . A real circus.

Of course I had chosen a great spot for watching—they all drove right past me. Just in case, I put Frosya on the roof of my Volvo and pulled my feet up onto the stump I was sitting on.

The truck drivers called out to me in every language, but I paid no attention. I was waiting for "my" truck. And it came.

Just as I was getting worried, I saw a mammoth blink its headlights and heard it give three beeps. I looked at the license: ABE 51–15. Sovtransauto!

"Vitya!"

51–15 pulled out of the flow and drove up to me.

He jumped down from his high cab and picked me up from that stump. And he didn't let me down. He held me in his arms, like a child, and I kissed his neck, his face, his eyes . . .

○

An hour later we were in the deserted terrace of the cafe I had taken him to the first time.

Once more our vehicles stared at us through the window, once more Frosya was under the table. This time we drank only coffee, and I was as sober as a bell. A round loaf of black bread from Leningrad lay on the table.

"Your neighbors are out of town."

"I know."

"Their daughter is vacationing in the south."

"My, my!"

"This kid is helping out Alla Sergeyevna—running errands to the store. And helping around the house."

"And who's that?"

"Nice kid. Around sixteen. Her pupil, Kozlov, I think."

I almost fell out of my chair. "Kozlov! I don't believe it!"

"He's a nice kid. He's like a protective wall for her."

The waitress came over. "Anything else, madam?" She stared at the bread.

"More coffee?" I asked Vitya.

"No, thanks. Time to go. I have another five hundred kilometers to Goteborg."

"Oh, stay another second," I asked. I spoke to the waitress in Swedish. "Could I have a carton of your best American cigarettes? And do you have disposable lighters?"

"Yes, madam. What color?"

"All of them."

"There are ten to a pack."

"The whole pack, then."

"Excuse me, madam. What is that?" she asked, pointing to the bread.

"Russian bread," I said and laughed.

"Does it taste good?"

"Very! Want a taste?"

"No, no, thank you. I'll bring the cigarettes and lighters."

She left and we sat in silence. I loved him in a way I had never loved anyone else in my whole life. And I told him so.

"I love you the way I've never loved anyone else in my whole life."

"It's the same for me," he said. "Exactly."

"Damn it. Where were you?"

"How about you?"

"I was so deep in shit that I'd rather not remember."

"Then don't."

"I can't help it. Something always reminds me."

The waitress came back with the cigarettes, the lighters, and the bill. I paid, put the black bread in my purse, picked up Frosya, and we headed for our cars.

"Give this to Kozlov," I said, handing Vitya the cigarettes and lighters. "I'm not sending anything to Mama,

I'll be there soon. The package in your cab, that's for my father—the address is on there. He has trouble with his feet, they're always cold. It's some warm socks and some clothes for his kids. All right?"

"No question."

"Forgive me for burdening you with all this, but you're the only link . . ."

"Quiet." He kissed me tenderly, protectively.

I thought I was going to faint.

"Get into your truck," I said hoarsely. "I'll accompany you for ten kilometers or so as far as Sedertelie. I'll stop at the fork, but you keep going to Goteborg. I'll wave to you. That will be better."

We flew down the highway, passing everyone. I was in front.

When there was a clear section of road, I'd slow down and pull up next to him on the left, so that we drove side by side. As soon as anyone came toward us, I pulled ahead of him back into my lane.

And then, at the crossroads, I pulled over and stopped. And got out of the car.

Vitya slowed down, blinked his lights at me, honked at the highest power, and roared past me with a scary rush to his idiotic Goteborg for some stupid spare parts, damn them all!

I was sitting at the bar at the gas station, sipping my pineapple and coconut juice and watching Reya work.

"Take me on as an assistant," I said casually.

"And we'll take a Danish princess on as dishwasher, right?" Reya said and laughed. "After Larsson was promoted to department chief of his company, you can only become owner of your own company. Your position requires it!"

"I don't give a shit for that position."

Reya pulled out the telephone. "Will you call Edward?"

"No. I'm not in the mood."

"Too bad. I like listening to you talk Russian."

I did get to talk in Russian. And not on the phone, but face to face. And not how I would have liked, either.

When I got home, I literally didn't know what to do with myself. I even spanked Frosya for barking. And then I found the phone book and called Vera from Moscow.

Vera picked up so fast it sounded as if she had been waiting for a call. The instant I dialed the last digit. It scared me.

"Hello, Vera? Hi! It's Tanya Larsson from Leningrad. You know, Zaitseva, Tanya. Remember me?"

"God, Tanya! I was just thinking of you."

I had a lump in my throat—I wanted to be sitting and talking with her so much.

"Come on over, Vera," I said. We'll have a drink, sing a song. Come on over. Please."

"Tanya! I'd love to. With all my heart. But I was just heading out the door. I've taken on this thing, remember I was mentioning it? I have to leave town for a week. I'll come right over the minute I get back. You can't imagine how happy I am that you called!"

"Too bad," I said. "I'm feeling so blue today."

"Don't be sad, Tanya! Keep your tail up! When I get back, we'll have a real girls' night out! That's it, Tanya! Gotta run."

And I heard the dial tone. And then Edik came home from work.

To keep from falling apart completely, I started a major clean up and dragged the howling vacuum cleaner all over the house, while Edik tried patiently to watch the TV news.

My vacuuming bothered him, his presence bothered me—we were both irritated and didn't even try to hide it. Our nerves must have affected Frosya—she raced around the rooms barking.

"Why do you have to clean the house in the evening?"

he asked reasonably, trying to be heard over the vacuum, Frosya, and the TV.

"Because I was busy earlier!" I shouted, working around the floor vase filled with dried grasses.

"Then could you do the upstairs first and let me watch the news?"

All I felt like doing was sending the upstairs and the downstairs, and the vacuum, and him to hell. I wanted to be sitting in the cab of the big Volvo truck, with Frosya on my lap, looking at Vitya's big strong hands on the wheel, and driving to Goteborg with him, a place I'd never seen.

"No way!" I shouted like an idiot. "First I'll clean downstairs! Why can't you clean out your shaving brush once in a while!"

I ran into the bathroom, grabbed the brush, came back and threw it down on the table between him and the TV set.

He jumped out of the armchair, ran into the bathroom, and came back with a tube of shaving cream, which he threw onto the table, too.

"No one asked you to wash it! I run through the tube twice as fast because of you! And that costs money!"

The vacuum cleaner was on, Frosya was barking, the TV was droning . . .

"That?" I laughed as insultingly as I could. "You call that money? It's a piffle!"

"It's not a piffle, it's money that makes up our lives!" he shouted and waved his arm to encompass everything around us.

"In that case, I hate this life!" I yelled, furious, and knocked the brush and tube of shaving cream off the table.

The brush and tube shot across the room, as if out of a slingshot, and hit the curtain. The curtain moved, something clicked, and fell to the floor . . .

. . . and the shotgun went off!

The big vase was shattered and the dried grasses fell all over the floor.

I screamed and ran to Edik. He held me tight and stared at his own shotgun on the floor.

I don't know how I could have forgotten it there.

O

"I don't know how I could have forgotten it there," I said, sobbing.

I was on the bed, covered with a light blanket. I was shuddering. It was quiet. The TV and vacuum cleaner were off, and Frosya was lying at my feet.

Edik was next to me, holding a cup of hot tea for me.

"Why didn't you tell me sooner?" He looked over at the gun, now unloaded and on the table.

"I didn't want to upset you."

"I'll go to the travel agent tomorrow and get visas and tickets to the Soviet Union. No matter what it costs. If you want, we'll go to Leningrad, if you want, Moscow, if you want, the Black Sea. Whatever you want!"

"Leningrad. To see Mama."

"Okay! Leningrad it is. To see Mama. And now, Fru Larsson, I invite you to the most expensive restaurant in Stockholm!"

O

The restaurant really was terribly expensive. It was part of a fashionable nightclub, they served amazing

131

dishes, and we drank a divine Spanish wine, and danced and danced. I wore a long evening gown, Edik a tuxedo.

He chattered like a student, made jokes, laughed, and was surprisingly generous. I had never seen him like that. I was rather quiet, looking around, and according to Edik, was a full ten!

After one in the morning, tired and wan, filled with tenderness and gratitude to each other, we left the restaurant and came out on the cool street to get our car. It was the nicest evening in my life in Sweden.

This was the only part of Stockholm still awake: bars, cafes, stores, and movies were all open.

As we were getting into the car, I saw a big white sign over a small movie theater across the street, illuminated by a bunch of bulbs: "Five Days of Russian Film."

The show must have just ended. People were coming out, but not moving away. Instead they were waiting near a small van. Flashbulbs were going off.

I looked into the crowd and recognized Gundareva, Smoktunovsky, and Leonov!

I was stunned. Amazing! They were here in Stockholm!

"Oh, Edik!" I shouted. "Look, look! That's Gundareva! And Smoktunovksy! And Leonov!"

"Who are they?"

"Our best movie stars! They're superstars!" I was thrilled and I rushed across the street with a shout. "Hello! Hello! My God, is it really you?"

Smiling tensely, the actors looked at me, looked at one another, and then at their "keeper," a sturdy little toad of a man in a white shirt and tie and dark suit. He must have been from the embassy.

The man heroically blocked access to the actors with

his broad back and addressed me severely in Russian. "Who are you? What do you want here?"

Fool that I am, overjoyed to see Russians, I didn't pay attention to the police tones in his voice, and just babbled on. "I'm from Leningrad . . . I live here . . . I married. I'm Russian! Russian. This is wonderful! Hello! Oh, God, I'm so happy!"

"Excuse us, madam, we are in a hurry," the little man said and shouldered me away professionally. "And, comrades, please get in the van. Get in, get in."

"You ought to be a doorman at the Evropeiskaya or the Astoria! You'd be worth your weight in gold!" It was the old story, pick on your own to scare off the others. I stood in the middle of nighttime Stockholm in a stupid evening gown unable to understand what the hell had happened. Why?

Getting into the car, Gundareva, who must have been a good woman underneath it all, smiled sympathetically at me. Leonov looked guilty and uncomfortable and gave the embassy creep a dirty look. Smoktunovsky, however, looked blissfully unaware, it had nothing to do with him, and calmly got in.

And then I got so mad. I saw red, and I shook furiously, and I screamed so that the whole street could hear.

"I'm Russian! Russian! I loved you so much, you damned bitches! You cheap clowns! I loved you! Why did you avoid me? Who are you afraid of? You should be afraid of him, not me!" I kept pointing at the embassy guy, in his white shirt, tie, and dark suit.

The van drove off. Edik took me by the shoulders, tried to calm me down, mixing Swedish words with Russian ones, as he tried to get me into the Turbo SAAB.

○

We drove slowly to our little burg. In silence. Quiet music came from the radio. I smoked one cigarette after another, breathing in the warm, fresh air of the Swedish white nights, and not thinking about a thing. But I really wanted a drink.

As we approached our house, Edik pushed the remote control and the garage door swung open. The lights went on. We drove in. As he helped me out of the car, Edik kissed the top of my head and said quietly, "I love you very much, Tanya."

I sobbed and wailed. "Then nothing can scare me."

"It's going to be wonderful weather today," Edik said, shutting the garage. "This evening we'll be able to . . ."

I thought, if it's the same weather in Leningrad, Gulliver and Kisulya will spend the day at the outdoor pool at the Dynamo sports complex.

○

I had always known that they had to catch you red-handed for an arrest under Article 88, "violating the regulations on currency operations." You have to be doing a deal when they grab you. You get three to eight. I had only heard about it. God had spared me the personal experience. But I would find out what can happen when I heard about the fate of my friends back home.

Kisulya and Gulliver were on the empty stands around the pool, their gym bags with them. They had done their swim and now were watching the little kids in the kiddie pool and talking with two of the coaches, handsome young men.

Kisulya looked at her watch, slung her bag over her shoulder, and said, "Why don't you stay and chat, Sima? I'll be right back."

She went down behind the stands and out into the sunny parking lot. Went over to her car, lit up, and looked at her watch again.

A beat-up old Moskvitch pulled up next to her sparkling Zhiguli. Kisulya looked around—was anyone watching?—and got in the back seat.

The driver of this marvel of technology was none other than Petr Nikanorovich, the hotel doorman!

Kisulya handed him a fat envelope. Petr Nikanorovich looked inside, saw the dollars, and said, "How much?"

"As we agreed." Kisulya was nervous.

"Take this." He handed her a pack of rubles.

"Turn off the engine, I can't breathe."

"Don't tell me what to do." Petr Nikanorovich looked around the parking lot, the exit from the pool, and the tall bushes by the gate. But he didn't turn off the engine.

Kisulya put the packet of money on her lap and started counting.

"Are you nuts?" the doorman hissed. "Is this the time?"

"Last time you were short two hundred, you old bastard, and now you think I should trust you?" Kisulya was mad.

Just then the front doors were flung open on both sides and Tolya Kudryavtsev shouted, "Don't move!"

In the blink of an eye Petr Nikanorovich tossed the envelope with dollars out of the car and stepped on the accelerator. Tolya and Mikhail Mikhailovich fell out of the car. The Moskvitch was going fast.

But a black Volga tore out of the bushes. Zhenya was at the wheel. He blocked the Moskvitch and took the hit directly.

○

Then there was an ambulance and another police car, which held Petr Nikanorovich in handcuffs.

The smashed Moskvitch and Volga were steaming.

They were carrying Zhenya away, bloody and very pale . . .

Kisulya was running next to the stretcher, wailing, "Zhenya, it's not my fault! I didn't want this to happen! It's all his fault! Him! Not me, Zhenya!"

Tolya Kudryavtsev brushed off his jacket and was cleaning his trousers.

"Shut up, you bitch," he said in a low voice. "You're the only one at fault. If it weren't for you, he wouldn't exist." He pointed at Petr Nikanorovich in the police car. "And Zhenya would be fine. Wipe your snot and get in the car. Help her, Misha."

○

When I called my mother in Leningrad just a few days later, I knew nothing about this.

"Mama! Darling, can you hear me? Listen closely!" I shouted into the phone. "Edik bought me a trip to Leningrad. For the end of the month. No . . . No seats before that. Unfortunately, he can't come. No . . . He's head of a department now, and the company won't let him leave Stockholm for a while! No, no! Everything is fine! Just fine! Ask Kozlov what I can bring him from Sweden. What a great teacher you are. What a change in that kid. How are you feeling? Great, thank God."

○

I could visualize things at my mother's end of the telephone. Mama was sitting up in bed and her skinny arm was in a blood-pressure cuff.

The doctor from the ambulance was patiently waiting for our conversation to end.

An electrocardiograph was on the table. The nurse was filling a syringe with Kordiamine.

Kozlov was smoking in the kitchen.

"Sima called the other day. I said, Sima! Nina is having some sort of trouble . . . No, I don't know what. Sima said she would call you. All right, dear," Mama said. "Don't worry. Send my love to Edik. I kiss you, too. I said, I kiss you and can't wait to see you. Goodbye, darling. Goodbye."

Mama hung up the phone and looked at the doctor guiltily.

"I'm sorry. But it was a long-distance call."

"Alla Sergeyevna, we have to do another cardiogram," the doctor said.

○

"Mama sends her love."

"Thank you," Edik said politely. "I think it would be better if she called us, rather than we called her. It's much cheaper there. And then we can pay her back at the exchange rate."

"What?" I didn't understand.

"I said that international calls from Russia are much cheaper than from Sweden. Your mother should call us, and then we'll pay her back."

"God!" I was incensed. "Go to hell! When will I make a human being out of you?"

When Vitya got home, he was searched at the Vyborg customs.

They found my parcel for father, opened it and started in.

"If these aren't your things, then why didn't you put them in your declaration? There's a special section: 'Articles or valuables belonging to others.' "

"I forgot all about them! How can you call these valuables?"

The customs agent was looking at two pairs of heavy socks, children's clothes, and a package from IKEA addressed to my father in Leningrad.

"You cross the border twenty times a year! Is it so hard to remember the customs regulations? Today you bring in somebody's socks illegally, tomorrow videos with anti-Soviet films, and the day after tomorrow you'll bring in pornography, eh?"

"Just don't try to build a case against me," Vitya chuckled.

"I'm not planning to do anything. Take your stuff and go along. You'll have to explain to your bosses what you're bringing to whom from whom . . . Goodbye."

Two weeks later, when it was time for Vitya's next trip to Sweden, I was very worried and tried to get Edik off to work early, so that I could get myself ready and off to the Viking Line port.

I twirled in front of the mirror like a girl, changed clothes ten times, and even spanked Frosya to keep her out from under my feet.

I checked the Sovtransauto calendar three times (with Vitya's arrival date circled in red) against the big kitchen calendar. I was a wreck.

This time I reached the port by a different route. I had lots of time, so I rolled up to the only Russian Orthodox church in Stockholm. I had been wanting to stop by for a long time, but I couldn't get up the nerve. But today I was drawn to that church by a powerful force!

I got out of the car, looked at myself in the mirror,

powdered my nose. As if I wanted to look decent before the Lord.

The doors of the church were open and cool air came from inside. Votive lights in front of the icons flickered in the gloomy space.

I stood in the doorway and couldn't force myself to cross the threshold. I sighed and went back to the car.

Exactly at nine I was at the port, on my "stump," with Frosya on the car roof.

Large and small cars poured out in an endless stream from the ferry. But I needed only one car from that stream.

And when it showed up and I saw the oval sign that read Soviet Union and the number ABE 51–15, I began hopping up and down and waving my arms!

But this time the Volvo truck didn't leave the stream. It moved slowly behind a French truck, not paying the least bit of attention to me.

I shouted, "Vitya! Hey, Vitya!"

The truck was passing close to me and with horror I saw a total stranger, an elderly man, at the wheel. And another man in the passenger seat.

"Wait! Wait!" I shouted in confusion. "Where's Vitya? Comrades!

The driver pointed me out to his pal and said something.

I waved harder. "Comrades!"

Without slowing down, the driver opened his door, stared at me, and said, "We're no comrades of yours. Whore."

He slammed the door in my face and drove on.

My God, I got so drunk on the terrace of that cafe where I had been twice with Vitya.

My lonely Volvo was parked outside.

My faithful Frosya sat on the dirty, wet table, whining and trying to lick my face.

The TV babbled away over the bar, the news showing pictures of disasters.

And suddenly a familiar face appeared on the screen. I raised my heavy eyelids, looked closely, and recognized Vera!

And the announcer's voice said, "Vera Gustafson, a Russian prostitute, who had been living in Sweden . . ."

"Greetings, Vera," I said, lifting my glass in her honor.

". . . was arrested while attempting to bring in several kilograms of narcotics. Preliminary investigation shows . . ."

I drank to Vera, picked up a heavy ceramic ashtray

from the table, and threw it at the screen. The glass shattered, there was a rather small explosion, and Vera's picture disappeared into a gaping hole.

The last thing I saw was the frightened waitress holding my purse and the cafe owner, who had taken out my documents, at the phone.

Then Edik showed up, all upset, in his SAAB, with Reya, the bartender from the Gulf station.

They dragged me into the SAAB, which was hard because I didn't want to go.

Reya started my Volvo, Edik his SAAB, and they took me home.

Telephone! Telephone! Telephone! Damn it! It was reverberating in my head. Drop dead!

I found the receiver and put it on the pillow next to me. I couldn't even open an eye.

"Well, who is it? What do you want?"

I was speaking Russian. And the voice in the telephone was speaking Swedish.

"Fru Larsson, a call from Leningrad. Soviet Union, Fru Larsson."

"Yes! Yes! I'm here! Mama?"

It felt as if cats had made a mess in my mouth. My head was splitting open.

"Mama?"

"Just a moment! I'll connect you!"

I looked around and saw that I was alone. Edik must have been at work. Frosya was sleeping on his pillow.

"Sweden? Salem?" The questions were in Russian.

"Yes! Yes!" I shouted, gulping down mineral water from the bottle. Mama?"

"Tanya! It's me, Gulliver. Listen to me, don't interrupt! They got Kisulya—with twenty-five hundred greenbacks.

At the very first interrogation she said the money was yours. Can you imagine? And that you had given it to her in front of me! When they called me in, I fell into total unconsciousness: I know nothing, saw nothing . . . She's trying to blame it all on you. Says you left the twenty-five hundred for her to exchange later and then give it to your mother in rubles . . . What a bitch. I thought she was going to bite my throat when they brought us together at the police station. Tanya, as soon as you come into the country, they'll arrest you. So stay put. Don't show your nose here!"

"But it's bullshit! Lies!" I shouted. Sima! You know that it's not true. I'll be there in a few days, and we'll . . ."

"Are you nuts?" Gulliver yelled. "You've got five years waiting for you. You'll go straight from the airport to jail. By the time you prove you're innocent, you'll have spent three years in jail. And remember, I'm not going to help you. I don't know anything about your affairs. Just stay there and be quiet!"

"But my mother is sick!"

"She'll get better. Would you rather have her come for visiting hours? Oh, by the way . . . Remember Natasha the Schoolgirl? She's got AIDS, the cretin. The doctors say its hopeless, she'll die soon. Well, that's it . . ."

"Wait, Sima!"

"I said that's it!" And she hung up.

○

What should I do? What should I do? What should I do?

"What should I do, Frosya?" I shouted, grabbed the dog, and shook it like a rag doll.

Then I tossed her aside, grabbed the phone, and dialed.
"Edik! Come home! I'm begging you! Darling . . ."
"I'll be home by six. Please, don't have any alcohol."
"What alcohol? How can you think of alcohol? What are you talking about? I need you right now. I've never needed you so much as I do now. Edik, darling, my one and only . . . I'm begging you . . ."
"I can't leave during the work day. Can you get here to me?"

O

Uncombed, unmade up, dressed in grubbies, I rushed down the Salem-Stockholm road, and oncoming cars scattered out of my way.

Probably, to the Swedish sense of propriety the scene we played out in the Belitronics parking lot was disgusting. Edik and I ran around our cars, slammed doors, grabbed each other, pulled away from each other, shouting, mixing Russian and Swedish words and behaved—for the business part of town—in a strange and indecent way.

"You're not going anywhere!" he shouted. "I'll have your visa and tickets annulled tomorrow! I love you too much . . . I don't want to risk it. And you have to change your citizenship immediately."

"And why is that?"

"You shouldn't be a citizen of a country with such crazy laws. The whole civilized world buys and sells currency—they have banks, stock exchanges, an enormous monetary system of relations among normal states . . . It's absolutely legal. But in your country, you're not allowed to do it. Why should a person go to jail for changing one currency into another?"

"They go to jail for speculation, not exchange! Can't you understand that?" I was defending laws that I had violated time and again in the last few years.

"I don't want to understand!" he shouted. "I love you . . . I can't live without you! We'll change your passport. You'll become a Swedish citizen and those laws won't affect you."

"What about Mama?"

"I'll make sure that Mama moves here, to be with us! It's possible now—even your people are writing about it. Just don't leave me . . . Don't go there . . . They won't let you out! By the time they figure out you're innocent, a lot of time will pass. I won't survive it. Do you hear me?"

"Edik! My mother is sick."

"We'll send her the best medicines! The most expensive. I know you don't love me yet. You just had to leave there. But I love you. I can't lose you. I'll do whatever you say. If you want to drink alcohol, drink it. I'm just worried about your health. Do you want to go to another country? To Australia? To New Zealand? It's always warm there . . ."

"My God, my God. What am I going to do, Edik?" To the amazement of the many Swedes who were watching us from windows and the sidewalk, we rushed into each others' arms.

Meanwhile, the vile creature that I was sat in her own two-story house, living off the fat of the land, a mere ninety-minute flight away from Leningrad listening to the heavy autumn rain bang on the roof and windows.

When the front doorbell rang, I looked out the window and through the dusk and rain saw the small car of the Salem post office by our gate and our mailman, Walter Muller.

I pushed the button to let him in, the gate opened, and Muller walked to the house. I met him at the door.

"Good evening, Fru Larsson," Muller said with a smile. "A telegram. From Russia."

"Thank you very much, Mr. Muller, thank you." I was agitated. I gave him a few crowns.

Muller bowed and I opened the telegram right there, without going in. In Latin letters it said, "Come. Mother sick. Kozlov."

The Swedish phone book was in front of me.

For the first time in the eighteen months I'd lived in Sweden I was turning to an official of the Soviet Union.

"Hello! Is this the Aeroflot representative? This is Tanya Zaitseva, a Soviet citizen. Actually my name is Larsson now . . . I'm married here in Sweden. Excuse me. I have a flight to Leningrad at the end of the month, and I have to leave today. Immediately. No, the ticket is on SAS. I just got a telegram, my mother is sick. They wouldn't send it if it weren't important. Please! And then I have another matter to attend to in the USSR. . . . Very important! Perhaps of state importance. A person has been slandered. And I'm the only one who . . . Of course! I'll make it! I have a car . . . Thanks! Thank you very much."

I hung up and began packing the first things that came to hand.

"My mother is sick, Frosya" I muttered. "Mother is sick. . . . We have to fly! You and I don't have the right to stay here . . ."

Ten minutes later I had dragged two heavy bags to the garage, stuck them in my Volvo, and pulled out of the garage. I locked all the doors, put Frosya in the car, opened our gates, and shouted across the street, "Fru Holstrom! Fru Holstrom!"

My neighbor ran out of her house in a raincoat holding an umbrella. "What's happened, Fru Larsson?"

I handed her the house keys and said, "Fru Holstrom! I know now that it is improper to borrow salt from Swedish neighbors. Impolite. But could you give the keys to my husband? Will that be very impolite? I'll leave the car at the airport."

"Of course, Fru Larsson, of course. Although, if you had called me on the telephone for me to come to the gate, you wouldn't have had to shout in the street."

"Right! That's what I'll do next time. Goodbye, Fru Holstrom!"

"Bon voyage, Fru Larsson."

It's only thirty kilometers from my house to the Stockholm airport.

I pushed my Volvo through the twilight rain, and the wet asphalt doubled the lights of the oncoming cars.

"Let them! Let them put me in jail. But they'll figure it out. The have the power and the laws!" I shouted to Frosya as I passed a truck. "They're not animals, they're people. 'What's twenty-five hundred dollars?' I'll ask. They always believed me in the vice squad. And that's no joke. They're part of the CID of Leningrad. And everyone knew me there! And everyone will tell you that I never lie . . . Yes, I had seven hundred-fifty bucks, which a Jap gave me. But you have to prove that I sold them!' "

The headlights were blinding me. Damn it. And that car in front was dragging its ass.

"Move to the right, you idiot! Don't you see me? Stupid! I'll be late! Thank God, you got the message!"

I pulled into the oncoming lane to pass a bus.

"Did the Schoolgirl really get AIDS? Can't they save the girl?"

○

I went into a slight skid in the wet, but I handled it well and without slowing down kept going.

"And then, Frosya, who knows that I'm coming today? Who? You'd think that the cops are just sitting around twenty-four hours a day waiting for me. Don't make me laugh. If they do notice me, it'll be two or three days later. And if Sima has even a drop of decency. . . . And then, when did it happen? A year-and-a-half ago! The hell with them all! Go prove it! Kisulya lied, and deal with her, leave me alone. I'm here to see Mama! My Mama . . ."

Another bus in front of me. I signalled, blinked my lights—they didn't care. I passed at high speed and almost crashed into another car. Good thing he went off the road.

"Ah, I feel sorry for Edik, Frosya . . . So sorry for Edik. Makes me cry. He was just starting to be a normal person. And then this. God! Look what happens—I love everyone, and they're miserable because of me."

I felt that I had started to cry. Tears filled my eyes and that made it very hard to drive. Rain and tears. Too much!

"But he has to understand that I must see my mother. They have different relations with their parents, but we Russians see it another way. If you have a mother, you have to see her as much as possible! Then nothing else is bad. Even if they arrest me at the airport, I'll say, 'Excuse me, if you are normal people, you have to let me be with my mother, at least for a day. I came especially to see her and I must see her.' "

I started to pass again, but just then a huge vehicle with enormous headlights appeared in front of me.

The blinding light hit me right in the eyes. I couldn't see anything and tried to brake. I skidded and the last

thing I heard and felt was a horrible squeal, a blow
. . . and flying through the air!

I flew into the darkness and shouted, "Mama, Mama,
Mama!"

POSTSCRIPT

Tolya Kudryavtsev was standing in the doorway of a rundown Leningrad apartment.

"Alla Sergeyevna, one last question. Not for the record. A personal one, if I may."

"Please," the old, deathly, woman said weakly.

"Did you really not know what Tanya was doing before she moved abroad?"

The old woman said nothing.

"How could you not suspect for so many years?"

"Do I have to answer?" she asked pathetically.

"No," Tolya said quickly. "As you like."

"You know, Anatoly Andreyevich, perhaps this will seem strange and unconvincing . . . But Tanya and I protected each other." The old woman paused and added. "A lot."

"Get better, Alla Sergeyevna. I wish you the best," Tolya said and went out on the stairs.

Kozlov and his gang of five came to the same driveway after Tolya Kudryavtsev's car left. Kozlov watched it go and then offered the kids American smokes. "Stay here. I'll go up and see what needs to be done."

The kids flopped down on the benches, pulled out their disposable lighters, and lit up.

Kozlov opened the door with his key and went in. An elderly woman was in the kitchen, looking at pictures of a young child.

"Who was that?" Kozlov asked suspiciously.

"Tanya's friends from her old job."

"Why does he have cop plates?"

"What did you say?"

"Nothing. Do you need any thing, Alla Sergeyevna?"

"If it's no trouble, could you go to the post office? Send Tanya a telegram. Here's the text." She handed it to him. "The words are Russian, but in Latin letters. Can you copy it over?"

"What does it say?"

" 'Feel fine. Postpone trip. Mama.' And the address."

"That's what I should put?" Kozlov clearly did not like the text.

"Yes. But in Latin letters. Here's the money."

"Fine," Kozlov said. "Then the guys and I wanted to go someplace."

"Fine, fine," the frail woman said.

○

At the post office Kozlov was behind a drunken man of about thirty.

There was no one else at the post office. Except for the young woman behind the semicircular glass with the sign: Telegrams and Transfers.

The man counted out three hundred rubles in tens and stuck the remainder, about two hundred, in his jacket pocket. He gave the woman a transfer form.

"Is it right now?"

"Now it's right." The girl started doing the transfer.

Kozlov's gang was outside, talking, and Kozlov could see them through the big window. He looked at the jacket pocket of the man in front of him with the pack of tens and moved closer.

"You have to pay for the transfer," the girl said.

"Sorry, sorry, sorry," the drunkard muttered and put his hand in the pocket.

Kozlov jumped back. The man pulled out a ten and slammed it on the counter. "Our pleasure!"

Kozlov carefully removed the remaining money, neatly hid it under a pile of telegram forms and casually began reading the various announcements on the walls.

The drunk got his receipt and change, and trying to walk soberly, went out. Kozlov watched him through the window. He crossed the street and got into a waiting taxi. He left.

"Are you just going to stand there?" the woman asked.

"Sorry, sorry, sorry," he said in imitation of the drunkard, and the woman laughed.

Kozlov folded over the piece of paper, leaving only the address and said, "Here's the address. International. Can you write in Latin letters?"

"Text?"

"Here it comes. Write: 'Come. Mother sick. Kozlov.'"

Kozlov watched the window, waiting for the drunk to come back.

"Three rubles sixty-two kopecks."

Kozlov gave her a five, got a receipt and change. He waited a second and looked out the window again. The man had not returned. His gang was smoking outside.

"Can I take a few forms?"

"You can have all of them."

"Thanks, you're terrific!" Kozlov took the forms and the tens and went outside.

"Come on!" he commanded and quickly went around the corner.

They stopped, he looked around, winked, and said, "A small trick, gentlemen!"

He opened the telegram forms and showed them the pack of tens.

"We're going to party boys! I got a transfer."

"Way to go, Kozlov!" The boys made their voices harsh.

O

The boys smoked once more on the bench in front of Alla Sergeyevna's house, while Kozlov ran upstairs to return the receipt and change. He took the steps three at a time.

On the third floor he slowed down and sniffed anxiously. He looked around, lifted a garbage lid. But the smell wasn't from there. It was coming from upstairs. Kozlov rushed up to the fourth floor.

The smell was so strong here that Kozlov started to cough, his mouth filled with burning saliva, and he felt nauseated. He realized that the smell was coming from Alla Sergeyevna's apartment.

He dropped the receipt and change and with trembling hands started to unlock the door. At last the key turned in the lock. Kozlov pulled the door open and recoiled—the gas was so strong!

"Alla Sergeyevna!" Kozlov shouted and, covering his mouth and nose, ran into the apartment.

The windows were shut tight. A lullabying hiss came from the kitchen.

Kozlov threw up. Wiping his mouth on his sleeve, he ran to kitchen and saw a lifeless form collapsed on the floor, the scattered photographs, the open oven door.

Choking and crying, Kozlov shut off the gas and pulled at the window. He was panicked and the windows wouldn't open. He threw a kitchen stool through the pane.

Fresh street air burst into the kitchen. With bleeding hands Kozlov grabbed the old woman by her robe and pulled her out into the corridor.

"Alla Sergeyevna!" gasping and weeping, Kozlov called to her. "Alla Sergeyevna! Help me somebody, you bastards! Help!"

He dragged her out onto the landing and started ringing doorbells and banging on the doors with his fists.

"Help!" he shouted and cried. "Somebody help! Come on, you bastards!"

No one opened. It was daytime . . . Summer . . . And it was too late, anyway.

"Help. . . ." he whispered and sank to his knees next to the woman.

There was no false hoarseness in his voice, no street

savvy. Gone was the leader of a gang that steals cars at night, deflowers girls in cellars, and is ready to beat up any strong adult male.

Next to the frail, skinny, elderly woman sat a frightened fifteen-year-old boy, and his body shook with sobs and horror, because it was the first time he had seen with his own eyes the death of a human being.

ROLLING OVER, THE SMALL VOLVO 343 CROSSED THE MEDIAN DIVIDER, BROKE THROUGH THE METAL GUARD RAILS AND STRUCK FOUR CONCRETE PILLARS UPROOTING A HIGHWAY ADVERTISEMENT FOR GULF GAS STATIONS.

IT HIT WITH SUCH STRENGTH THAT TWO PILLARS COLLAPSED, THE LIGHTS SPARKED AND WENT OUT, AND THE CRUSHED VOLVO BLEW UP, BURSTING INTO FLAMES IN THE TWILIGHT. . . .

On a warm white night in sleepy Leningrad, through open draw bridges with their lampposts floating in the pale sky and trolley tracks upended, a small tugboat pulled a huge barge with clean yellow sand down the Neva.

The little island of sand with its shores defined by metal moved slowly past embankments with signs saying "Do Not Drop Anchors."

. . . past the translucent gratings of the Summer Gardens . . .

. . . the buildings of different times and eras . . .

. . . and the enormous Intourist Hotel with cars sleeping under its awning . . .

O

On the fifteenth floor the hard currency bar was still open for tourists.

Opposite the entrance, at a small table with two elderly Englishmen sat the glorious Sima Gulliver in full battle gear. She listened closely, laughed delicately, looked smart . . . A dream, not a woman!

But she looked up, seemingly accidentally, at the entrance, and her face was transformed by a smile.

In the doorway, hand raised in greeting, stood the incredibly beautiful Lyalya.

She was dressed elegantly and expensively—with that small touch of calculated vulgarity that is perceived not as a lack of taste but as a sign of professionalism.

"Hello, gentlemen!" Lyalya said.